Solstice Surprise

GABBI GREY

A *blizzard, an urgent plea, a desperate journey, and the most important moment of their lives.*

Action movie star Peter Erickson is spending the Christmas holidays ensconced with his in-laws and his new husband. In the wilds of Northern British Columbia, they are as far away from the bustle of the city as they can get.

Thomas Walsh and his famous husband are deeply in love. Although he prefers the intimacy of their city house, he's come home to face the reason he left ten years ago, and to finally tell his parents the truth.

A desperate phone call has the couple scrambling. Will they get back to Vancouver in the middle of a snowstorm in time for their solstice surprise?

Contents

1. Chapter One   1

2. Chapter Two   12

3. Chapter Three   24

4. Chapter Four   38

5. Chapter Five   51

6. Chapter Six   73

7. Chapter Seven   86

8. Chapter Eight   93

9. Chapter Nine   104

10. Epilogue   114

11. Interested in knowing more about Gabbi?   126

Chapter One

Thomas

My first Christmas at home in ten years. I should have been more excited, right? Okay, I was excited. But why was I freaking out? My family had met Peter before. Heck, they loved Peter almost as much as they loved me. It didn't faze them in the least that he was one of the biggest stars in the movie industry. They treated him like family. Hmm, he was more at ease with them than I was.

"You're doing it again."

I glanced over at Peter. I wouldn't ask what he meant. Yes, I was overthinking things. Stressing. Worrying about nothing. My handsome husband leaned over to press a kiss to my lips even though we were sitting in the living room of my parents' modest home in Prince George, British Columbia.

"Why don't we go for a walk?"

Dubiously, I stared out the window. The dead of winter had come to Canada, and we were far enough north that daylight was at a premium. The stark grays and browns hadn't been softened by white yet, but the weather forecast was for heavy snow tonight. Possibly even blizzard conditions. A pleasant night to cozy up to the gas fireplace and spend time with the ones I loved. My sister Sarah was in her room texting her best friend from university and my parents were out doing some last-minute shopping.

At December twentieth, they didn't have much time left. Peter and I had flown up yesterday with extra luggage filled with all the gifts. We'd gone overboard, but this was our first Christmas as a married couple. My family weren't likely to be wooed or impressed by expensive gifts, but Peter and I had chosen a few things that would hopefully bring smiles.

"A walk sounds nice." Such a banal word. "But we'll need to be home before dark."

"Is there a park around here?"

"I was thinking the woods. There's a nice place just out of town. Kind of secluded." In other words, Peter shouldn't be recognized, although he didn't mind—or so he said. Truth was, I thought we both needed a break from the celebrity thing. He'd attended all those charity events leading up to the holidays, and he was fatigued, even if he'd never admit it. Being up here was just what he needed. Time to recharge. Time to center himself. Time for us to be together. I didn't mind him doing so many events, but the studio had been shooting the second season of *Vigilante Justice* until three days ago. I'd seen more of Julie Reyes and Cole Hamilton than I had my own husband.

"Secluded sounds perfect."

He rose gracefully and offered his hand. I grasped it and let him pull me up. When he wrapped his arms around my waist, I went willingly.

Nothing better in the world than Peter Erickson hugs. I was taller by a few inches, so when he ducked his head, it fit right under my chin. His scruff rubbed against my cheek and mine was rubbing against his. Scruff looked sexy on him, and I encouraged him to keep it. On me? Yeah, not so alluring. But after all the eighteen-hour days, the mere thought of shaving made me tired.

"I love you." The words slipped easily from me. They were as natural as breathing. He knew, of course. But we never took each other for granted. Never wanted the other to feel unappreciated. In fact, he loved me so much he'd accepted my formerly feral cat Calvin, the orange tabby, into his life. He'd even hired a house sitter so the cat wouldn't feel lonely. I'd thought a service to visit every day was enough, but Peter insisted Calvin not be lonely. One more reason why I loved him.

"I love you too."

He released me and we headed to the closet in the front hall so we could get our coats. As I was putting on my jacket, he caught me off guard by putting a scarf around my neck, and before I could protest, he'd stuck a hat on my head. "Hey." I frowned at him. "It's not that cold outside. It's, like, minus five."

"In English, please."

I did some quick mental calculations. "Twenty-three."

He shivered.

I laughed. "You're such a Texas boy."

"Via California," he reminded me.

"Well, you're in Canada now." He was applying for Canadian citizenship. Our marriage was expediting the process. "You need to learn Celsius."

"I need to be in warmer climes."

Again I laughed. "Usually this time of year it's about minus fifteen or even twenty. Today is warm."

He growled. Then grabbed for a cap.

I was quicker and I snagged the cap for myself and stuck the tuque on his head. He looked adorable. Adjusting the cap, I waited while he wound the scarf around his neck and snagged gloves.

"You have yours?"

I didn't, so he handed me a pair, rolling his eyes. He was adorable when he was in protective mode. Most of the time we were on equitable footing despite our fourteen-year age gap, but sometimes I let him think he was in charge.

All an illusion.

I snagged the keys to Sarah's SUV, and we headed out into the nippy air. I'd never had to ask permission with her. I admired her *whatever is mine is yours* philosophy and tried to emulate that trait.

I disarmed the alarm—truly something unnecessary up here—and Peter hopped into the passenger side and slammed the door. I was a little slower in getting in.

"It's freezing."

"Quit grousing." I snickered. "This walk was your idea."

"Don't remind me."

The engine turned over, but I needed to plug in the vehicle when we came home. Was supposed to go down to minus twenty-five. Probably a good thing we were taking our walk today. No way my SoCal man would venture out tomorrow. Jacking up the heater, I pulled out of our driveway and headed down the street. The place I was thinking of wasn't far out of town. Bears were hibernating this time of year, and seeing other creatures was unlikely. Not that I'd say such a thing to Peter. He could handle a huge horse like nobody's business, but bears terrified him.

Go figure.

"You spend a lot of time out there?"

A memory flashed. "Yeah, Luke and I went out there quite often. Sometimes his friends would join us, but just as often it was the two of us."

"I'm sorry." His words were quiet.

"They're wonderful memories." And they were. I grasped Peter's hand. "I'm better at remembering the good times. Those remembrances don't hurt as much as they used to." Because of Peter. Admitting to Peter what had happened to me the night of my brother's death had lessened my burden. I still planned to tell my parents, but my heart raced every time I thought of trying to. They never blamed me for Luke's death, but I'd spent ten years blaming myself. Letting go of that guilt was hard. Even with the loving support of my husband.

Husband.

My heart still soared whenever I heard that word. I'd been in the closet when we met. Hell, so had he. A paparazzi outed us. Best thing that'd ever happened to me, although it didn't seem so at the time. We played fake boyfriends at first, but later became an actual couple. Within days I'd known he was my soulmate, and I'd been the one to propose after we'd been together a mere month. An early autumn wedding meant we were now approaching our three-month anniversary. Wow, time was flying.

Pulling into the parking lot, I swung into a spot, yanked up the parking brake, then cut the engine. After patting Peter's thigh, I hopped out.

He was much slower to get out.

"What's taking so long, old man?"

Another growl.

He hated being reminded of the age difference. So I did it several times a week, in jest, of course, trying to desensitize him. We had yet to have our first proper fight. Not that I relished the idea. More that it was an inevitability. My parents loved each other, but even they bickered once and awhile.

We met at the front of the SUV and I held out my hand. He reciprocated. Better if it was skin to skin, but in deference to the weather, we'd keep our gloves on.

The path was well-used and the snow compact. Our winter boots made us well-prepared. A shiver ran through Peter and I yanked him close. "You sure you're up for this?"

"They've offered me a film role that'll shoot up in the Yukon in February. That's near Alaska."

As if I didn't know that. My shoulders tensed. "When were you going to tell me?"

"The offer came in yesterday morning, just before we left for the airport. I meant to tell you on the plane but, honestly, I forgot."

"Have you accepted?" Not that he owed me a vote, but it'd be nice if he'd consult me.

"Before talking to you?" His voice was incredulous. "Of course not. I told them I'd give them an answer after Christmas. I think I should turn it down."

This would be the first role he'd taken since our marriage. I was done shooting *VJ* and hadn't agreed to anything else for a while. I had planned on some alone time before... "Oh."

"Yeah, oh."

Now we were on the same wavelength. I hated the thought of him giving up this role, but we had bigger plans. The timing was off, so maybe it wasn't meant to be.

I squeezed his hand. Could he feel that? Then he squeezed back, and I could breathe again.

As we ventured farther into the forest, the path narrowed. Would we see anyone today? Usually not, but I couldn't be sure. As we passed a large tree, Peter tugged me off the path and into the snow. What...?

"Up against the tree. Face me."

Oh, that tone. His bossy tone. His *I mean business* tone.

I obeyed and pressed myself against the tree. I flashed back to the scene this past summer in Whistler. He'd been fucking Cole Hamilton against a tree much like this one. Of course, it'd been a warm day with an entire film crew watching. But now? We were isolated, sure, but people might stroll by. And my cock was likely to shrivel if out for too long.

Peter grabbed my hands in one of his and held them above my head. The height difference meant he was straining against me, our bodies pressed together. When his erection pressed against my groin, my own sprang to life. With his other hand, he yanked my chin down and our mouths met. Joined. Fused. And like it always was, ferociousness reigned supreme. Soon I was pressing against him, seeking friction. Too much denim, goddamnit.

Then he released my hands.

"Keep them up."

"Yes, Sir." We didn't have a BDSM relationship per se, but he loved it when I obeyed. And when it was my turn to flip the table, so to speak? He'd turn into a submissive partner, willing to relinquish control. Infrequently, though. I rarely felt the need to dominate, and he seldom felt the need to cede control.

"You have a smart mouth. If it wasn't so fucking cold, I'd punish you for it."

By filling it with his cock.

Damn, why did it have to be so chilly?

He yanked off his gloves and shoved them in his pocket.

Uh-oh, something was up. He made quick work of the button on my jeans and he deftly lowered my fly. His hand had only been out of the glove for mere moments, but it was bloody cold as it encircled my dick. I hissed out a breath. "Jesus."

"Oh, you'll be praying to a deity soon."

Like that, was it? As he pumped my shaft, I did say a little prayer to God. Partly that it would be over soon. Partly that it would last forever. Mostly that we not have unexpected company.

"Kiss me."

With pleasure. Our mouths fused again in a bruising kiss and it was only a matter of time. Electricity shot through me and my blood heated. He pressed his thumb against my slit and twisted in just the right way. Pulling back from the kiss, I gasped for air, needing to fill my lungs. The sharpness of the cold temperature plus my warm breath created a white puff.

I wanted to hold out. Really. But he commanded "come", and I did. Spectacularly. I would've cried out if he hadn't joined our mouths together again. He smothered and absorbed my shout of joy. When he pulled back, his sea-green eyes sparkled. I'd never get over their color. Stunning in their intensity, his pupils were blown and his irises were darker than normal.

"You're amazing."

I was warm and glowing despite the weather. His praise always comforted me, especially when we were coming down after an orgasm.

"You haven't..." I could barely get out the words.

"Blue balls never killed me."

I laughed as I flashed back to the first morning of shooting on the film where we'd met. I'd sat on the ground to maintain the power imbalance while Peter and Cole had sat on chairs. I'd quipped something about blue balls and Peter had laughed. Making him laugh was one of my favorite things to do.

He slid his hand out of my underwear and gave me a quick nod.

I zipped myself up quickly. The cold air was in sharp contrast to my heated skin.

"Lick."

I did, sucking on his fingers as I licked my cum. He'd taught me this. How to appreciate the taste. How to revel in the act's carnality. How to hang up my puritan notions and embrace my sexuality.

The crunching of snow jarred me out of my sexual haze. I glanced over Peter's shoulder.

Two women rounded the corner on the path. Their steps faltered.

"Uh..." Words utterly failed me as my cheeks heated, undoubtedly turning scarlet. And if the ladies had been in any doubt of what we'd been doing, my flushing was confirmation of it.

"Lovely afternoon." The taller woman with a blonde ponytail spoke. Her blue eyes sparkled with apparent amusement. She wasn't wearing a hat.

That was crazy, was my incongruous thought.

"You gentlemen look like you're enjoying the outdoors." This comment came from the shorter woman with brown hair. Her brown eyes also showed good humor.

Peter subtly adjusted his jacket so it covered his erection. The erection that was soon to flag.

Or at least I hoped it would.

He turned to the women and let loose his megawatt smile. "My husband and I were just enjoying nature. I'm not from around here, so he was explaining about the different trees."

Trees? Seriously? That was the best he could come up with?

"Yes, our trees are unique." The blonde's brow arched. "Where are you from, exactly? If you don't mind me asking."

"Not at all. Texas via Southern California."

A nanosecond later the women exchanged glances.

Wait for it...

"Peter Erickson." This time the brunette spoke.

"That's the name my parents gave me." He turned on the charm. "I would offer to shake hands..."

The blonde held up her hands. "No, we're good." She glanced down at the other woman. "This is my wife, Shelby. I'm Lark."

"Two lovely names." The line could've been cheesy, but somehow Peter pulled it off with no effort. "This is my husband, Thomas."

Lark gave me an appraising look. "I was in the same grade as Luke. I remember you, but as you were then. Didn't recognize you with the scruff."

In other words, I had finally grown up.

She offered me a sympathetic smile. "I always liked your brother. He was one of the good guys. I was devastated when he died."

My chest squeezed, the breath whooshing from my lungs. *Say something.* "Thanks. He was a great guy. I miss him every day." Okay, so not too lame.

Peter looped his arm around my waist and gently pulled me toward him. Marking his territory by being protective. A classic move if ever there was one. Calm settled over me.

"We're heading back into town." Shelby inclined her head. "You gentlemen interested in getting a hot chocolate or coffee at Louie's?"

Man, I was tempted. Louie's made the best hot chocolate in all of Prince George. I looked down at Peter, meeting his gaze. He was giving me permission to decide one way or the other. He'd honor whatever decision I made.

A chance to talk with someone who knew Luke? A person outside of my family? We might mention Luke in passing, but we rarely had entire conversations about him. More than ten years on and it still felt raw. "Hot chocolate sounds delicious."

Peter pressed a chaste kiss to my cheek. Unconditional support. He always had my back.

Chapter Two

Peter

Thomas never ceased to amaze me. My husband's inner strength had grown with each passing day. I wanted to believe it was a testament to our love, but it was more than that. The decision to join Lark and Shelby for hot chocolate was a show of strength and maturity because we both knew this was going to wind up being a discussion about Luke.

He drove us to Louie's, and we arrived just as the women were pulling up. "You sure you want to do this?" If he said *no*, we would turn around and go right back to his parents' house.

He patted my thigh but exited the SUV wordlessly.

Well, I'd given him the chance. We approached the café, me with trepidation and him with, I believed, inner resolve. He'd changed a bit since we left Vancouver yesterday. When we were out in public, he didn't take my hand. Aside from when we were on the trail—where we were unlikely to encounter anyone—we'd been more like friends than lovers. Of course, anyone who looked closely would be able to see the matching wedding bands.

Thomas had once confided that Prince George, PG to the locals, had been homophobic when he was growing up, but he had no idea how it was these days. His parents were okay with him being gay, so that was all that mattered to him. Given Lark and Shelby were holding hands, there was clearly some tolerance in town. But then, aside from my time in LA and Vancouver, I found lesbian couples ofttimes faced less prejudice. Something about two men and what they must be up to in their bedroom made some people uncomfortable.

Lark whispered something into Shelby's ear, then took off to nab one of the remaining two tables. She shucked off her jacket and sat.

I nudged Thomas. "Why don't you go join her?"

He hesitated, then did as I suggested.

Shelby glanced over her shoulder. Spotting me, she smiled. "I take it you're up here because of Thomas and not some movie thing."

"Correct. Thomas' family lives up here, and we wanted to spend the holidays with them. Low-key, as it were."

She tapped her index finger against her lips, then she spoke with clear deliberation. "I'm half a dozen years older than Lark, but when she mentioned how Luke died, I remembered. One of those events that made an impression, you know? PG is still, in some ways, a small town." She eyed my ring. "You guys should be okay."

"More tolerance?"

"Sure. I mean, not everyone is raising a rainbow flag, but you'll find support in some surprising places."

"Fair enough." I rubbed my fingers against my ring. I often caught myself doing so unconsciously. I'd been in the closet for forty-two years. The fact I was out—and had a husband—felt surreal. A feeling I never took for granted.

The customer in front of us departed, and Shelby stepped forward, placing her order. I offered to pay, but she gave me a haughty look and tapped her card. So much for chivalry. Many women weren't interested in that anyway. Equality was important, and I'd do well to remember that.

She moved on and I smiled at the young man at the cash register. He couldn't be more than sixteen.

"Oh my God."

Okay, apparently old enough to have seen my movies. I was known for my summer blockbusters despite having done some brilliant artistic roles as I'd been cutting my teeth in the industry.

He flapped his hand excitedly. "You were in that gay movie with Cole Hamilton. I've watched it, like, ten times. What's Cole like to work with? Is he as gorgeous off camera as he is on?"

His words caught me off guard, but I smiled. Obviously, Lisette Grenier's little film about two gay men had reached more than just the art houses in major cities.

"Cole is amazing to work with." I pointed to my husband. "Thomas works on *Vigilante Justice* with Cole. He can tell you stories."

Not that Thomas would tell anything more than the most innocuous ones, of course. He valued his job too much to do otherwise.

The kid—Cameron, according to his name tag—grinned. "Could I get your autograph? For my mom? She's a huge fan. It disappointed her when you first came out, but now she's good with it. Something about seeing you happy." As I signed the paper he handed me, he leaned in. "I'm hoping you smoothed the way for me, you know?"

I did know. Had received hundreds of letters from young men and women—and some older ones as well—that they'd found the courage to come out because of me. Because of my relationship with Thomas. Because of my marriage. I had done none of those things for anyone other than myself, but knowing I'd helped people made a difference to me.

Flipping to a second piece of paper, I wrote out my email address. "In case you need anything," I said to Cameron.

His eyes widened as he registered what I was doing. It was my public account, but I still didn't go around handing it out to everyone I met. He carefully tucked the note into his pocket, grinned at me, then pointed to the other end of the counter. "Your order will be up shortly."

I gave him a tip of my hat, belatedly remembering I was wearing the tuque and not the cap I'd tried to steal from Thomas earlier. Yeah, I looked cheesy. But my head was warm and that was what really counted. Moving toward the end of the counter, I arrived just as Shelby was being handed one coffee and one hot chocolate. She hesitated, and I waved her on.

Taking the hint, she headed over to the table.

Momentarily alone, I pondered on how life worked. Simple little decisions could have profound consequences, while huge ones could have little impact. Clearly the gay love story movie I'd been in had changed this man's young life. If he found the courage to come out, then it'd all be worth it.

The middle-aged woman passed me the two mugs, and I thanked her and made my way over to the table. Okay, how was Thomas faring? His back was to me, but his posture was rigid. Not a good sign. I placed the mug in front of him and sat next to him.

He wrapped his hands around it.

I draped my hand over his back, gripping his shoulder. Instead of relaxing into the grasp, as he usually did, he continued with the stiff countenance. Should I remove my arm?

He reached up to touch my hand, letting me know I'd done the right thing.

"Thomas was just telling me about the movie industry in Vancouver." Lark's eyes were lit with obvious interest. "He says it's not nearly as glamorous as it's made out to be."

"He's not wrong on that count. It's plenty of hard work and lots of hurry up, get ready, wait around." I grazed his cheek with my palm, enjoying the scratch of the stubble. "Thomas will never admit this, but he's one of the best personal assistants in the business."

He snickered. "Well, that's an exaggeration. My boss puts us all to shame." He took a tentative sip of his drink. "Now, I don't need to tell you how great Peter is."

Was I blushing? Even after twenty years in the business, I still was uncomfortable with praise. Plus, a small part of me believed Thomas was obliged to say nice things about me because he was my husband.

"But he hates me saying so," he was quick to add.

"We saw the romantic movie that came out recently. We might have both cried." Shelby linked her arm with Lark's and leaned against her. "We're suckers for any good love story. But a gay one? With a bittersweet but happy ending? All the better. We need more representation. You taking that role made a statement."

More than she probably knew. It'd propelled me out of the comfortable closet I'd been living in all my life. Even the death of my secret lover hadn't been enough to convince me that coming out was possible. One intimate photo with Thomas hitting the internet had changed everything. As he liked to say, fake boyfriends to the real thing in the blink of an eye. Even that first night I'd been intrigued. He had odd ice cream preferences and I'd been hooked.

"You know all about us, what do you ladies do?" A lazy question, to be sure, but one that was socially acceptable.

"I'm a sports coach and Lark's a firefighter. She works for our city department but often deploys to other countries to handle forest fires. She's done two seasons in Australia back-to-back."

"And the volleyball team Shelby coaches won the provincial championships for the second year in a row."

Pride shone in both the women's expressions. This was, undoubtedly, how I gazed at Thomas when recounting something special the younger man had done. Sometimes words were inadequate to express how proud I was of him.

"It's the kids who do the hard work." Yet Shelby grinned from ear to ear.

Yeah, this was something she was proud of, and rightly so.

"Firefighting is a tough job." Thomas' voice was quiet. "There aren't always happy endings."

"No, there aren't." Something bleak passed across Lark's expression, but it was gone just as quickly. "But we chalk up the successes and try to focus on them. A bit of counseling thrown in always helps." She took a sip of her coffee. "Growing up, I knew I wanted to help people. In my teen years I focused on medicine. In the end, I wasn't cut out to be a doctor. I studied to be a paramedic then came back up here and joined the fire department. It wasn't easy, I can tell you that much. But totally worth the hard work. I love my job."

"In a profession that hasn't always been welcoming to women." Thomas nodded.

"Very true. I lucked out. I got an excellent captain who watches out for me while never giving me preferential treatment. I work hard to maintain my physical fitness and consistently hit or exceed targets set for me."

"This is her being modest." Shelby grinned. "She's third from the top in her department and she's on track to make assistant chief within five years. Would be the youngest female yet."

"That's great." I championed women in an industry still dominated by men. Lisette Grenier, one of the top directors in the business, was the reason our film had been so successful. Okay, and maybe all the shots of me naked with Cole Hamilton. Not that the sexy man was my type any longer. No, I was all about tall brown-eyed men with shaggy hair.

Of course, when production for *VJ* ended three days ago, Thomas had headed to the barber for a nice close crop. I'd eventually get used to the new look. His cheekbones were more prominent now, and his eyes less likely to be hidden by the long hair I loved to grab and yank while we were making love.

Okay, wrong thought. I gave my cock a stern talking to. I might be forty-two, but any carnal thoughts of my husband always got my libido going.

"What's your next project, Peter?" Shelby's expression was open and curious.

"We have something in the works in our personal lives that may preclude me working for some time to come. Truth is, I've enjoyed my downtime. We're looking at several scripts for a sequel to one of the blockbusters I starred in. I want the story to be solid before I commit that kind of time to the project. And, of course, it'll have to be shot in Vancouver."

Thomas took a sip of his hot chocolate to hide his smile.

I had more than enough money to last several lifetimes, even with the generous donations I made anonymously. But I liked working. If the right project came up—and if it was in Vancouver—I'd sign up. But Thomas would always come first. Plus, with the exchange rate being what it was, producers were still flocking to British Columbia to shoot their films.

I'd also seriously considered doing work behind the camera. I wasn't convinced I had the aptitude for directing, but the idea of producing appealed. Just something to keep busy. I loved my charity work and my husband, but I disliked being idle.

"Luke was one of the reasons I went into firefighting as a profession."

Lark's quiet words completely derailed my train of thought. Had I missed something, or had this been the young woman's plan all along?

Thomas stiffened, wrapping his hands around his mug, undoubtedly seeking the residual warmth from the long-consumed beverage. "Luke was a good man. He was the best brother anyone could've asked for." He swallowed audibly. "I wish he was still around, but I know it just wasn't meant to be."

Thomas wasn't a fatalist per se. More of a realist.

"He was in most of my classes." Lark smiled, fondness in her expression. "He always made me laugh. He always made me think. He was top in the class but never lorded it over people. In fact, he was always willing to help out anyone who asked."

"Yep, that was him." Thomas' words were quiet.

Lark nodded. "He'd challenge me, often pointing out where I could do better. I used to think it was high-handed of him. Only later, in retrospect, did I realize it was so I could see my own potential." She swallowed audibly. "He made me want to be a better person. I admired him so much. When he died…" She tucked a wisp of hair behind her ear. "I grieved. We all did, I suppose, but I remember feeling like part of me had died with him. That spark of joy left me for a long time.

Eventually I moved past the pain, but it took time. Going south for my paramedic training helped. You know, getting out of PG for a fresh start."

"We…" Thomas coughed. "We were only eighteen months apart. Just one grade. I was always hanging around him, you know? And with his friends. He never tired of me. Not once did he tell me off or try to stake territory as his own. He just added me to the group, and we were all really close."

"Do you ever see the guys? Who were they? Colin and Jeremy and…" Lark tapped her lips.

"Bartholomew."

"Right." She laughed, a rich-throated sound. "He hated that name but hated 'Bart' even more."

"Something about *The Simpsons*, if I remember correctly." Thomas grinned. "My dad's name is Bart, but he came long before the show. He's kind of embraced the whole thing."

She snapped her fingers. "Of course, I'd forgotten that."

Thomas stilled. "I don't see the guys. Without Luke…it'd just feel wrong."

Unexpectedly Lark reached across the table and touched his hand. "I know they wouldn't feel that way. Jeremy went to the oil sands in Alberta as an engineer and no one's heard from him since, but Colin has a forestry job in town, and Bartholomew teaches first grade."

A sputter escaped Thomas. "Bartholomew? The guy who was six-three in ninth grade? The giant?"

"The gentle giant." Lark's tone was soft, her smile warm.

"True." Thomas scratched his head. "He freaked out when they had mice in the house and his mother set all those traps. Good thing she had the constitution to clear those traps, because he never could've done it."

"His mother had a stroke last year. She's in an assisted care facility in town."

"Aw shit."

I knew the exact emotion Thomas was enduring. Guilt. He always carried way too much, and I was irrationally angry at Lark for having heaped more on him.

"She's doing okay. Just can't live on her own anymore. Bartholomew's living in her house and dating a nice young woman from the church who moved to town recently. I think he's smitten."

Thomas relaxed a fraction. "Yeah, I always knew he'd make a good husband and dad. So caring, you know?"

"I do."

Shelby cleared her throat. "We have news of our own." She exchanged a long look with Lark before turning back to us. "I'm almost three months pregnant. We used a sperm donor we found online, and I went down to Vancouver for the treatments. It took on the first try and we're optimistic."

"And it's twins." Lark's eyes watered. "I'm the one who is so scared. Shelby's all tough and sure nothing bad is going to happen."

"But you've seen things can go wrong." Thomas' sure words had Lark nodding. If anyone understood her fear, it was him.

"We're not telling anyone until the New Year when we'll be firmly in the second trimester." Lark pressed a kiss to Shelby's temple before turning back to us. "But it feels right to share this with you. Especially because if one twin is a boy, we're going to name him Lucas."

Holy shit, now I was choked up. What were the odds of us all running into each other today of all days? And of the women being able to share such amazing and generous news?

Lark gazed back at Thomas. "I want to tell your parents when the baby's born. You don't think they'll be upset, do you? I mean we don't have to—"

"No, please tell them." Thomas' words came out in a rush. "That would mean so much to them. You know they'll shower the baby with love, right? They are such amazing people..."

"We know." Shelby squeezed Lark's hand. "It's why we wanted to let them know."

"I think..." Thomas cleared his throat. "I think part of them broke that day, and I think this could help heal them."

I wanted to argue. Thomas had held himself apart from his parents for the past ten years, believing if they knew the truth of what'd happened that awful night, they'd blame him. But in the short time I'd known the Walshes, I knew nothing could be further from the truth.

Again, Lark reached out to Thomas as if it were the most natural thing in the world. "You clocked out of town pretty quickly after graduation, and I know you rarely come home. But you'd make time to visit if you were an honorary uncle, right?"

Thomas blinked several times, but it didn't stop the lone solitary tear from escaping his lashes and rolling down his cheek. "You don't even know me."

"We do." Shelby laid her hand next to Lark's, covering Thomas' larger one. "We know how close you were to Luke. We know you've become a man your parents are proud of. Most of all, we think you'd be a wonderful role model if we have a little boy."

"Or a girl," Lark was quick to add. "This honorary uncle role crosses gender lines."

"Even nonbinary." Shelby's eyes shimmered as well. "We just want two healthy babies."

I wanted to assure them they would, but I couldn't say that for sure. But this peace offering to Thomas would go a long way to healing the young man's heart. No, not so young. Twenty-nine years encompassed a lot of living. But his breathtaking naïveté had been one thing that'd spoken to me more than words ever could.

"I accept."

Thomas glanced at me, seeking reassurance I was happy to offer.

"But you realize we come as a package deal."

"Oh, we understand." Shelby giggled. "But being a big-shot Hollywood movie star is not getting you out of diaper duty."

I wasn't sure there was anything I wanted more in this world.

Lark glanced at her watch. "Crap, we've got to run. I'm on shift tonight." She and Shelby rose and reached for the used mugs.

I placed my hand over hers. "We can take care of these." Now that Shelby's abdomen was at eye level, I could see the miniscule easy-to-miss baby bump. To think, there were two little beings in there. It always had the ability to blow my mind.

The women waved goodbye and headed out, holding hands.

Without warning, Thomas turned toward me and burrowed his face into my shoulder. I wrapped my arms around him, uncaring of who saw us. My husband was in pain and I'd do my best to bring him comfort. I could only hope it was enough.

Chapter Three

Thomas

If fat flakes hadn't been coming down hard, I would've offered the keys to Peter. And he would've taken them without question or hesitation. But he was from the southern United States and this was northern Canada in the dead of winter in what was shaping up to be an epic snowstorm.

I'd already asked so much.

Like my unspoken request that he hold me while we were in the café. In front of people he didn't know. While I quietly sobbed and got snot all over his brand-new and very expensive winter jacket.

Yeah, like that.

I needed two hands on the wheel, but he laid his hand against my thigh as I drove, struggling to see out the windshield. The wind had picked up and the snow was blowing sideways. Good thing we weren't far from home.

"Crappy night for Lark to be working."

There. I'd said her name without breaking down again. I had vague recollections of her, of course. But I didn't remember her being that tall or that gorgeous. Heck, she was taller than Peter—almost as tall as me. Shelby was shorter and felt sturdy. Not stocky, just sturdy. She'd make a great mom. They'd both be amazing mothers. Hopefully as good as mine had been. I'd lucked out in that respect.

So had Peter. But his parents died in a car crash when he was in his early twenties. They'd never seen his star rise and hold a pinnacle. I suspected, from what he'd told me, they would've been so proud.

"Hopefully there won't be many calls." Peter didn't sound like he believed that would be the case.

On a night such as this? Car accidents and drunk drivers were likely to abound. For all the progress we'd made with campaigns to stop drinking and driving, we were a long way from fixed. The truck driver who had hit Luke's car hadn't been drinking. It'd never been clear why he crossed the center line. Some momentary distraction, perhaps. Whatever the reason, it cost Luke his life. And robbed me of the rest of my teenage years. I was the reason Luke had been behind the wheel that fateful night. If not for me, he'd still be alive.

And Peter would kick me if he heard me saying any of this. Months ago, after I told him the entire story, I had promised to stop obsessing. And I had. Until coming home. I would always be here and remember what happened to my beloved big brother. My parents had made the choice to redecorate his room a few years ago so it didn't become a shrine to their lost son. That being said, I'm not sure any of us went into the room. I know I never did.

I pulled into the driveway and killed the lights and the engine at the same time.

The interior light came on just as Peter reached out to cup my cheek. "We can deal, you know. And we can always bow out gracefully."

"No." The word came out more forcefully than I'd intended. "I just didn't expect that level of generosity from a woman I barely remember and one I don't know at all. I knew…" I swallowed hard. "I knew Luke had impacted plenty of people in his brief life. I know you think I put him up on a pedestal, but he kind of belongs there. He was one of those truly selfless and caring human beings."

Peter grazed my jaw with his fingers. "I've said no such thing. I respect how much you love your brother. I'm just asking that you respect yourself as much."

Easy sentiment, so hard to put into practice.

The snow was already covering the windshield, leaving us shrouded in darkness. My family lived farther out of town than many, so no close neighbours, little in the way of local traffic. Here, in this vehicle, we were in our own bubble. Able to keep the world at bay for just a bit longer.

"I love you." The words came unbidden from me, pulled by some invisible force.

"Oh, sweetheart." He leaned over to place a gentle kiss to my cheek. Difficult given we were still both constrained in our safety belts. He shifted away and undid the seatbelt buckle.

After a moment, I did the same. I put my gloves back on and got out of the SUV.

Within moments Peter was beside me and we were making a beeline for the covered porch.

Sarah stood in the doorway, her arms crossed. "Were you making out in my SUV?" There was no malice in her teasing. "Come on in, it's freezing out here."

She was right. The temperature had dropped precipitously, and the snow was heavier than ever. We followed her back into the house, hit by a wall of warm air as we stepped into the foyer. Peter unzipped his jacket, but I stilled him with my hands. Slowly I brushed the snow from his jacket then unwound the scarf and pulled the hat from his hair. The static from the friction had his hair standing on end. I'd forgotten how dry it was up here compared to down on the coast.

When he moved to reciprocate, I batted his hands away. "Go freshen up, I can smell dinner." And I could. The most mouthwatering aroma of beef, garlic, and other spices permeated the house, and I thought there might be some baking scents in there as well. As I removed my winter garments and hung them up, I salivated. Mom's cooking really was to-die-for and was probably what I missed most since I'd moved away.

Aside from my actual family members, of course.

Peter was coming out of the guest bathroom as I headed in. That brisk walk in the woods had done us both good, and the hot chocolate had soothed something within me. I still reeled from our discussion with Lark and Shelby. It still felt unreal—like it'd happened to someone else. Or like Luke had been there in spirit with us.

And since I wasn't a spiritual person, that was perhaps the weirdest part of it all.

Taking care of obligatory bodily functions, I splashed cold water on my face. Uh-oh, I still wore my boots. Man, Mom was going to kill me, especially if I'd tracked slush and snow into the bathroom. I followed my trail back to the foyer and saw nothing. Peter's boots now sat on the mat, so he'd had the same thought. I quickly removed my boots.

There were few rules in the Walsh household, but one was to remove all foot coverings at the door. Well, Sarah could get away with flip-flops in the summer, but that was it. Even Dad's sandals had to come off. Mom kept a tidy house and ran a tight ship.

My husband stood outside the kitchen. I cocked my head, and he reached for me, pulling me in for an infamous Peter Erickson hug. Oh, man. The first day of rehearsal, he'd hugged Cole Hamilton, and the embrace was the most natural and most erotic thing I'd ever seen. Possibly the first time I'd ever seen two men embrace in real life, in fact. When it'd ended, Cole had flippantly said how it was nice to meet Peter. It blew my mind. How could two men be so intimate with each other, so free with their emotions, and not know each other?

Part of me had mentally kicked myself, they were, after all, actors. Another part of me, though, had known I'd just witnessed something special. Something transcendental. Something earth-shattering—for me, at least. When we discussed it months later, Peter said he felt safe in Cole's arms, welcomed in a way he rarely felt. Well, that was how I felt every time he embraced me. Like something special. Like coming home.

"I think it's time."

He whispered the words in my ear and, despite myself, I stiffened. I knew what he meant. What he was conveying. His never-ending and unstinting support. And if I never shared my truth with my family, he'd support that. But this was a burden I'd carried for too long, and the time had come to release myself from the twin talons of grief and guilt.

I tucked my head against his neck and inhaled deeply. Peter didn't wear scents. but I could sniff the soap and, incongruously, cinnamon.

Maybe that was just Mom's cooking.

"You boys can set the table."

Ah, so not as secret as I'd thought. But then she always had eyes in the back of her head.

I guided us to the dining room where I opened the china cabinet.

Peter cocked an eyebrow.

"You're a guest. We always use the good china when it's a guest."

His look of hurt nearly broke me. "Uh, Mom, we can use the regular plates, right? The ones for family?"

Mom poked her head into the pass-through. She glanced between the two of us. "Of course, dear. Just make it quick in the kitchen, I don't want you in the way."

Needing no more encouragement or instructions, Peter and I headed into the kitchen where I carefully counted five place settings.

Five.

A gut punch, to be sure. I couldn't remember a single time since Luke's death where there had been five of us. Hoping my mother wouldn't catch my momentary hesitation, I raided the silverware drawer and again counted out everything we needed. Finally, I nabbed five glasses, and after Peter took them from me, I filled the carafe with water and added ice cubes.

Once I was back in the dining room, I opened the drawer and pulled out five of Mom's favorite Christmas cloth napkins and five placemats. Luke, Sarah, and I bought them when we were still young, saving up our allowance to surprise her. I think that year we got Dad another fishing rod. He and Luke had loved fishing while I'd been too squeamish. They'd never teased me about it, though, just made sure our weekends were also full of hikes and bird-watching that didn't require killing creatures. There were plenty of hunters up here, but my family were not, thank goodness, inclined that way.

"Where do I sit?"

Peter's quiet question hit me low in the gut. "Here." I pointed to the seat next to me.

"Was that...?"

I nodded, unable to speak. How was I ever going to get through this meal?

By using some of the grit Luke instilled in me. In retrospect, I wondered if he'd known his time was limited because he'd dedicated so much of it to me. Making me more independent. Stronger. Better, as Lark put it. Those early life lessons he'd instilled in me were still there. Although I had run from home, I found my way to Vancouver, joined the industrial alliance union for the movies, and worked my way up. I was now working for a major studio with a great-paying job, amazing benefits, coworkers I adored, and a boss I both feared and admired. Just the way she liked it. Yeah, Janine would be proud.

Dad entered the dining room first, carefully transporting the roast. He placed it in the middle of the table. "You boys sit, your mom and I will be in shortly."

Before I could protest or even offer to help, he was gone.

Peter's hand at my back guided me to my seat, and he encouraged me to sit.

"We set the table. If your mother wanted us to do more, she'd let us know, right?"

Of course, he was right. Peter was always right. Well, maybe not *always*, but pretty darn close. Yet he never lorded it over me. He would gently and kindly explain how to do something without making me feel stupid. And there were things I could teach him. Like how to become friends with a previously feral cat.

Most of the furniture in our home had withstood Calvin and his known temper issues. I'd come to adore the cantankerous feline. Fortunately, the curmudgeon had wormed his way into my husband's heart as well. In fact, Peter'd been the one to suggest getting another animal. Might be fine now while he wasn't working, but once he signed on to a project, there was no way to juggle more responsibilities. Plus, I had a strong suspicion Calvin wasn't the type to share nicely.

Moments after we were seated, Sarah breezed into the room bearing a dish of warm green beans and a basket full of fresh-baked rolls. She plopped them down, re-entered the kitchen, and came back moments later with a bowl full of mashed potatoes.

Man, Mom had gone all out on this meal. And we were still four days away from Christmas. At this rate, Peter and I would need wider seats on the plane home.

Dad arrived with the steamed broccoli, and Mom was last in with the cheese sauce. When they sat, my mother smiled. "I am grateful to have my son and his husband home for Christmas this year. I hope it'll be repeated often."

Crap. No guilt there.

"I'm grateful Thomas returned my SUV in one piece," Sarah intoned. "I understand city slickers in Vancouver forget how to drive in snow."

Forget? Not likely. Get a lot of practice? Uh, no. At least not until Peter had insisted on buying me a car. Public transit had been fine for ten years, but my husband was adamant I needed my own set of wheels. Needed? No. Was it nice? Well, I sure wasn't running the car back to the dealership anytime soon.

"I'm grateful I'll be retiring in June."

Wait, what? Dad loved his job. Had sworn he'd do it forever. Was this a forced retirement or...? "Dad, are you okay?" Oh, no. Maybe something was wrong, and I'd missed it because I'd stayed away so much.

"I'm fine, Thomas." Dad smiled. "Your mother and I have decided to do some traveling, so it seemed like a good time to hang up my hat. Plus, we plan to spend more time down in Vancouver."

Something I'd always wanted but wasn't ever sure I'd get.

Dad winked. "Your turn."

"Uh, yeah." Regroup. "I'm, uh, grateful for the bountiful and plentiful food." Okay, cheesy much? I was about to assure Peter he didn't need to partake in our ritual, but he was already smiling.

"And I'm grateful for this amazing meal, the wonderful company, and the fact this will be my first white Christmas."

Well, kick me in the nuts, that hadn't occurred to me. Of course, SoCal via Texas didn't lend itself to much snow. How hot was the average LA temperature for Christmas anyway? I made a note to google it.

Dad had already cut the roast, so it was just a matter of passing around the plate of meat and selecting a slice. I might have picked the one with the most fat. Mom always disapproved but held her tongue. It was our little secret. Luke used to take the piece that looked the toughest. Man, could that kid chew.

Sarah heaped potatoes on her plate and passed the bowl to our dad.

"Sheesh, Sarah, did you leave any for the rest of us?"

Her eyes lit. "Of course I did." Then she leapt from the table and headed to the kitchen, coming out with the gravy boat. "We almost forgot the best part."

Dad handed me the potatoes.

I scooped some on to my plate while Sarah smothered her food with the savory gravy. My saliva glands were working overtime.

Soon enough, we all had our plates piled high.

Mom smiled and said, "Bon appétit." Mom, Sarah, and Dad all dug into their food.

I nudged Peter and gave him a wink. His responding grin was a thing of beauty.

We consumed the meal at a leisurely pace.

Mom recounted an anecdote about a recent trip to the grocery store.

Sarah animatedly talked about one of her university professors. The woman was brilliant in climate science and hopeless at everything else, including, apparently, remembering to wear matching shoes.

"So, a stereotypical professor?" Peter arched an eyebrow.

"Totally. I'm thinking about asking her to be my PhD supervisor."

"Don't you have a Master's program to get through first?" I was doing my best to keep up with my sister and her academic successes, but it got overwhelming at times.

"I told you, they're letting me combine the two programs so I only have to do one thesis. It'll shave a year off my studies."

Had she told me this?

"Perhaps you forgot to mention it to Thomas. You and I have discussed it, but I'm not sure you remembered to tell your brother." Again, Peter to the rescue.

Sarah's brow furrowed. "I could've sworn…" Her face brightened. "Right, you and I were talking about money and Thomas was working."

Suddenly the food felt leaden in my stomach. "Money?"

"You remember." Peter used tongs to put another couple of green beans on his plate. "I'm paying for Sarah's PhD. She and I were discussing whether she was going to stay in her current school or if she wanted to go elsewhere."

"I've decided to stay." She took a sip of water. "Peter's offer is generous, but I want to continue to focus on forestry, and the best way to do that is to stay where I am. I'll manage just fine with Professor Forgets-Everything."

I had known about Peter's plan to finance my sister's education. He'd declared it after the first time he'd met her. He knew genius when he spotted it, and this wouldn't be the first talent he'd nurtured. But possibly one of the more expensive ventures. I wanted to contribute but could offer little. Peter could cover all her costs without missing a couple hundred thousand. That was a rounding error in his world. In mine it was a couple of years of hard labor.

Peter placed his hand on my thigh, and the warmth immediately seeped through the denim. He was asking if this was okay. I gave him my bravest smile. He wasn't trying to buy my affection—he never had and he would never need to. He was just trying to make things easier for my family. This was likely one reason my father could retire. Because he no longer had to worry about Sarah's school costs.

Returning his smile, I placed my palm over his hand, marveling at the smoothness of his skin. He wasn't vain, but he believed in using serious amounts of moisturizer. I often wondered if using all that expensive goop was worth the hard-earned cash. His smooth skin assured me it was money well-spent.

"Thomas, dear, you've barely touched your meal, is something wrong?" My mother's blue eyes sparkled, but a frown marred her brow.

"I'm fine, Mom. The meal was amazing. Maybe even your best."

She dismissed my compliment with a wave. "All well and good, but I don't remember you eating so little food since..." She met my father's gaze. They both turned their stares to me.

Peter's grip on my thigh tightened.

Now or never.

"I, uh, there's stuff I haven't told you..." God, why did this have to be so hard?

"Do you want me to leave?" Sarah's voice held a note of uncertainty, reminding me how very young she was. Almost seven years my junior, she'd been the baby in the family. Always doted on by her older brothers, but never spoiled. She could've grown up bratty and demanding, but she was mature and insightful.

"You can stay." I wiped my brow with the back of my hand. Why was it so warm in here? Was the fireplace going in the living room?

"Take your time, Son." Dad's voice was low and soothing. "We've got all the time in the world."

Perhaps, but now the attention focused on me, and my discomfort grew exponentially. I looked desperately at Peter, but he offered only a smile and unspoken support. He wasn't going to do this for me. Couldn't do it for me. No, I was on my own.

"You know Luke was driving to pick me up the night of the accident."

Mom's expression softened. And Dad nodded slowly. Man, it was awkward looking back and forth between the two of them. Maybe I should've waited until we were in the living room when I'd be able to find a vantage point to see both of them at the same time.

Too late now.

"What you don't know is where I was or what I was doing." Out in a rush.

"That's true." Mom said the words slowly. "We assumed it was something you didn't want to share and frankly, at the time, it didn't seem important. I suspect we were wrong about that."

I'd always thought they were angry at me. If I hadn't been out late, then Luke wouldn't have been coming to get me. If he hadn't been coming to get me... Yeah, that circular thinking could get me going for hours.

"I was with a friend. Or at least I thought he was a friend. Okay, he was more just a guy I knew at school and he approached me and, you know, the next thing I knew I was at his house."

My father's brow furrowed. "I thought you were out with a group of friends that night and you somehow got separated and that's why you called Luke."

"No, none of that was true. I was going over to this guy's house to, you know, make out. And I was ashamed. I didn't want to be gay, you know? And I thought if I just went over there and we messed around and it meant nothing, that maybe I wouldn't be gay." I was babbling but there was little to be done about that now.

"You don't have to say any more."

Surprisingly, the words came from Sarah. For one horrifying moment I wondered if she knew from personal experience why this was so hard for me, but something in her tentative smile assured me it wasn't. She'd guessed, but not from personal experience. Or at least I hoped not.

"I do, Sarah. But thank you," I hastened to add. This time I used the cloth napkin to mop my brow. Why had I thought I needed a flannel shirt and a sweater? Just because my parents preferred the house to be cool didn't mean I'd needed to layer up so effectively. "So, yeah, we were, uh, messing around." God, please swallow me up into the earth. Something—anything—to not have to do this.

No divine intervention came, and given I wasn't religious, it was unfair of me to expect anything.

"He told me he knew what he was doing, and he'd make it good for me. I didn't really want to, but I'd gone over to his house and I figured it'd be no big deal." A long swig of water did nothing to quench the thirst or ease my parched throat. "I was a tall kid, but I wasn't bulky or strong. This guy was. I fought. You have to know I fought." Memories flashed before my eyes. The olive-green shag carpet in his parents' basement. The lingering smell of tobacco on the couch he had me pressed against. The scratchy fabric against my cheek as he held me down. I'd always believed I was strong. I'd never imagined someone could... Yeah, wrong on both counts.

"He raped you." Sarah's words were soft.

I met her gaze and held it for as long as I could before I looked away.

"I, uh..." *Shit*. "I asked him to stop and he didn't."

"Which is the textbook definition of rape," Peter said quietly. He'd always had my back on this one. From the moment I'd told him the truth, it'd enraged him. Then he'd pivoted quickly to completely and unconditionally supportive.

Mom pressed a hand to her mouth, but it didn't hide the gasp of pain. I couldn't even look at Dad.

And in the blink of an eye, it overwhelmed me. Became too much. And not enough. And just...

"I have to go." I leapt up from the table and ran to my childhood bedroom. The room where I'd cried many nights after Luke's death. Always in mourning of him, I'd lied to myself. Never for me and what else had been forcefully taken from me that awful night twelve years ago.

Chapter Four

Peter

The silence left in the wake of Thomas' departure was profound and uncomfortable.

Sarah speared a pile of mashed potatoes but then let it drop back to the plate where she shoveled it around with her fork.

I chanced a glance at Norma, who held her hand clutched against her chest. I might've worried about her heart, but she was a robust healthy woman, and the expression on her face wasn't physical pain. More like mental distress.

Bart was also flushed, but there was no mistaking the rage. Several moments passed before he finally spoke. "Do you know the name of the guy?"

I shook my head. "He refuses to tell me. Said it happened a long time ago, and he doesn't want to dwell on it. Doesn't want to relive it.

I think he's convinced himself he's put it in the past. That he's only looking at it in the rearview mirror, and that it doesn't have the power to hurt him anymore."

"I didn't raise my son to be a fool."

For a moment I didn't get his meaning. "No, sir, you did not. You raised a fine young man who is one of the most compassionate and caring men I've ever met. He's more sensitive than many, but he hides it well. He feels things more acutely—"

"He always did." Norma didn't smile as she so often did when reminiscing about her children.

I hadn't spent a great deal of time with her, but her pride in her children was always crystal clear.

"Luke saw it. He worried people would take advantage of Thomas' gentle nature. He tried... Toughen up is the wrong term. He tried to help Thomas develop a protective shield. A way to keep the world at bay when things threatened to overwhelm him." She sniffed. "How did I not see this?"

I wasn't sure it was my place to answer. "You were mired in your grief for Luke. Completely understandable. He also let you believe his pain was because of losing Luke. No one is to blame here."

"Except the son of a bitch who raped my son." Bart's coloring was hectic red.

Should I worry about his stress level? "I've asked, Sir, and he won't give me a name. You can try—" I hesitated. "—but I think that might make things worse. He just needs to know you love and support him. He feels intense guilt for having called Luke that night. He needs to know you don't blame him for what happened."

"Of course we don't." Sarah pushed her plate away. "That's such bullshit. Of course guys can be raped." She spat out the word. "I'd like to kill the fucking bastard myself."

That no one admonished her for her language spoke volumes. Thomas and I were from the film industry where swearing was a pastime. But neither of us would dare utter a foul word in front of Bart and Norma.

"You should be with him." Norma's gaze met mine. "He needs you right now. Tomorrow the rest of us will talk to him, but tonight he needs the comfort he can always count on getting from you." She pushed back from her seat. "And he also needs cake. I made his favorite, so you need to take two slices up to your room."

Our room.

The acceptance in this house for my marriage to Thomas was complete. Never had there been a single moment of doubt in my mind. Hell, I was starting to see myself as part of this family, even though it'd only been a few months since I'd first met them. I rose as well and started collecting the dishes. Wow, Thomas hadn't eaten much at all.

"Leave it, Peter." Bart's voice was soft but strong. "You go take care of my boy. You make sure he knows we don't blame him. Never have, never will." His voice broke on the last word.

I feared tears might come. They didn't and I let out the breath I'd been holding. Not because tears made me uncomfortable, but because Bart was a man who clearly prided himself on holding himself together.

I didn't want him to think there was something wrong with showing emotion. I'd cried plenty when my lover had died, but it'd been a private grief. Thomas' brutal honesty had shown me that sharing grief could be cathartic. I think I'd always known this, but it never really stuck. Until a young man walked into my life and changed everything.

I put the plates back on the table. Cleaning up would allow Thomas' family some together time without the need for words.

There was always a chance words might come, but there was something about ritual that could bring peace.

Norma presented me with two plates of Black Forest cake and two forks. "Try..." She cleared her throat. "I'll leave a covered plate for him. If he gets hungry later tonight, maybe you can get him to eat that as well. I'm always worrying about him."

"I think that's a parent thing."

The formidable woman nodded, drawing herself up to her barely five-foot height.

I'd known from the beginning I was going to like her. Anyone who helped raise Thomas into the man he was had to be a good person. "I love him."

Her eyes brightened with unshed tears. "I know you do. It's the reason I'm not banging on his door and demanding admittance. He'll share with you what he can't with us." She reached up to press a cold and clammy hand to my cheek.

Not the warm woman I was accustomed to, but understandable given the shock she'd just had.

"You brought Thomas back to us once. I'm quite convinced you can do it again."

She had more faith in me than I had in myself at this moment, but I was willing to try. Giving her one final nod, I headed to the stairs. Norma and Bart's master suite was on the ground floor at the back of the house while their offsprings' rooms were on the second floor on the front side. Sarah's was first, Luke's next, Thomas' at the end of the hall. During my tour yesterday Norma had shown me Luke's room. In case I needed somewhere to hang out, she'd said. The décor of the room made it clear they'd redecorated the room since its previous owner's death.

This house was so homey. Such a contrast to the Texas ranch where my parents worked that I'd grown up on. They never had enough money to own our own place, but we were happy with what we had. Once I was financially successful, I'd bought a succession of houses for myself over the years, including the sprawling mansion in Los Angeles where I never went anymore. I had no desire to go back there. Just like there wasn't a bone in my body that truly missed Texas. Thomas was my home. He was my everything.

At Thomas' door, I balanced the plates across my forearm and turned the handle. Unlocked, of course. Thomas had shown me the locks last night, in case the need overtook us. I didn't plan on having sex in his parents' house, but that would make it the longest we'd gone without since we'd first made love so, yeah, I understood why he pointed out the lock.

And I might have given him a hand job today to take the edge off his need. To lower his stress.

To give me blue balls.

Not that any of that mattered now.

The lamp by his bedside cast long shadows in the room, but I didn't move to flip on the overhead one. I placed the two plates of cake on the desk, along with the forks, and slowly made my way over to the bed. Lucky for us, it was a queen. Unlucky for me tonight because he was on the far side with his back turned to me. Undaunted, I pulled my sweater over my head and tossed in onto our open suitcase on top of Thomas'. Seemed we were both too warm.

I slid in behind him, giving him plenty of warning of my presence. Then I did what I'd done almost every night since the first night we'd shared a bed—I pulled him tight into me and spooned him. He was taller than me, so this was always an interesting action, but it brought comfort to both of us. I wanted to be his protector. His champion.

The one who held the world at bay. He liked being held. He enjoyed the security that came with this simple act.

As I pressed my chest against his back, he melted back against me. We fit. We always had, and God willing, always would. This man was my everything.

I'd sworn I'd never get involved at that level again after my last lover died a horrible death from cancer. Then I met this charming young man who saw me for who I truly was. He didn't see Peter Erickson, movie star. Well, he might have at first. But he also saw Peter the grief-stricken man. Peter, who'd had the life sucked out of him but still breathed. Peter the man who, with a lot of patience, might love again.

And I had. It'd taken very little effort on his part and, voilà, I'd found my soulmate.

"I'm sorry." He hiccupped as he said the words.

I pressed a kiss to the back of his neck that was still hot and damp. "For what?"

"For ruining dinner."

"Shush. You didn't ruin dinner. Dinner was perfect. And your parents and sister are in awe of your bravery. They understand, in their own way, that you've been suffering for years, and that holding in that pain was holding you apart from them. They've only ever wanted you to be happy. And I think you are happy. Understanding that happy is a relative term and—"

He pulled my hand from where it was resting against his chest, to his lips, and kissed the knuckles. "You know I'm happy. Sometimes too happy. I worry that if I relax and enjoy it, something might take it away from me. I don't think I could bear it. Losing you would kill me."

I pressed another kiss to his neck. "You know I feel the same way. And we both understand life is a crapshoot. We're both going to die. But we can also spend the next fifty years living fully and loving completely. Personally, I like that idea."

He laughed and sniffled. "You always understand me."

"Yeah, probably why we're wearing matching wedding bands."

"I need you to make love to me."

Okay, not what I had expected.

"I need you to fuck me. I need you to obliterate the memories. Excise them once and for all."

He tugged my hand even tighter and the edge of pain caused by his grip matched his edge of desperation. I didn't know how to deny him. I never had, and I never would. "Okay," I whispered. "I'll go grab a towel and you get undressed."

"I don't want to wait that long."

"Well I can't fuck you while we're both fully clothed, and as progressive and understanding as your mother is, I don't want her to find cum in the bed linens."

"I'll launder them."

"All the same, let me get a towel. And I need to undress. If we move fast, I can be inside you in less than five minutes."

He pulled out of my arms and leapt off the bed. He was already unzipping his jeans while I pushed my weary body up and rolled off the other side. I was still in excellent physical condition, but not as spry as I once was. After glancing over my shoulder to see how far he'd made it—pants were down and shirt was unbuttoned—I left the room quietly and headed to the bathroom. Norma had laid out a pile of fresh towels for us. I grabbed several, stopping to take a piss while I was there.

Man, it was a good thing I'd packed the lube. I'd been thinking we could rent a hotel room for an hour or two if we were desperate. Never had I imagined making love under his parents' roof. Now, weirdly, I couldn't envision anything else. He needed me in a way he never had before. Would I be enough?

I entered the room to find him lying on the bed. He'd pulled back the sheet and duvet and he was gloriously naked. And stroking his erect cock.

The tableau had me stopping in my tracks. Thomas was adventurous, to be sure, but there were still moments of shyness. He'd never been this brazen.

I'd worried about getting and maintaining an erection through such a tumultuous time, but I needn't have worried. My body reacted the way it always did when I saw Thomas nude. I put one towel over the desk chair and placed the other on the bed.

"You said five minutes." He growled the words.

I fumbled to unbutton my shirt. Yanking it off, I made quick work of my jeans, briefs, and socks. I trembled as I tore through the suitcase, desperate to find the lube.

"Looking for this?"

I halted my search and glanced up to see Thomas with the bottle. He'd opened it and now squirted some on his fingers. It took him mere moments to spread his legs so he could work his fingers into his hole.

Holy shit. As much as I loved prepping him, I found it even sexier when he did it himself. Mesmerized, I watched as he fingered himself. Stretching to where it had to burn. Sometimes he liked a little pain. Sometimes he liked a little tenderness. All the time he liked it when I was inside him.

He tossed me the lube and I slathered some on my cock. I crawled onto the bed and over him. His pupils were blown in the low light, barely any brown irises left visible.

"Fuck me."

"I will, sweetheart." My instinct was tenderness, but that wasn't what he either wanted nor needed. I positioned myself between his legs, lined up my cock with his hole, and entered him in one smooth move.

Perfection.

We'd done this nearly every day for six months—sometimes multiple times a day—and it never got old. It never felt anything but special. I was never anything less than reverential.

I moved and he moaned. Loudly. In our home we could be as loud as we wanted. And he was that. He never held back. But here? In this space? Well, his parents were on the other side of the house, and Sarah had made a joking comment about owning good headphones. Never had I appreciated my sister-in-law's consideration more.

Pulling back, I held myself still and then thrust in again. Our rhythm was as familiar to me as breathing, so it was easy to fall back into the feel of things. To go on instinct. Sweat trickled down my back and broke out on my brow. Thomas wrapped his legs around my waist, trying to draw me even closer. With each thrust, my balls hit his ass with an erotic noise that ratcheted up my arousal.

"Fist yourself," I ordered through gritted teeth. "I need you to come."

I was on the verge of orgasming and there was no way I was going over without him.

He did, spitting on his hand and then smearing precum along his cock. He was vigorous, and each jerk matched the rhythm of my thrusts. "Oh, fuck, Peter. I'm…"

The word left unsaid was also unnecessary as I felt the warm spurt of cum against my belly, and I watched as it coated his abs. Permission granted, I thrust a couple more times and came with my own growl.

Electricity shot through me, curling my toes and singeing my hair. Would it always be this fucking amazing?

I collapsed on him, mindful of his now-deflated cock. I withdrew and rolled onto my back, yanking him with me so he could cuddle against my side. He moved his leg so it lay over mine, entangling them. He pressed himself so his body was flush to mine, and so he could tuck his head into the cradle of my shoulder. Finally, he placed his left hand on my chest, resting it above my still-racing heart.

We were a tangle of sweaty bodies and the feeling of rightness settled over us. For me, this was the best way to enjoy the afterglow. Sure, we were still overheated and panting, but we were joined, if a little less intimately than before.

"I know I say this all the time, but that was fucking amazing." Thomas pressed a kiss to my shoulder, just above my armpit.

I tightened my grip against his sweat-slicked back, tugging him even closer. "You don't have to say that. Is it appreciated? Well, telling a man he's talented in bed is never a bad thing." In return, I kissed the top of his head, still surprised by the short cut. I'd become quite accustomed to his long hair. But this look was growing on me. Pretty soon I wouldn't be doing a double-take each time I saw him.

"I want to pull up the covers and go to sleep."

I laughed. "I do too, but we're both covered in cum. I'll get a washcloth and wipe us down. Unless you want a shower..."

"God, no. I'm not moving." He flopped onto his back and flung an arm over his eyes.

Neither of us enjoyed getting up in the afterglow, but both of us enjoyed the sensation of the warm washcloth cleaning us so we could cuddle again properly, sans cum.

Realizing that stepping naked into the hall wasn't the brightest idea I'd ever had, I slung the spare towel around my waist. With one last look at my exhausted husband, I opened the door to the hallway.

And ran right into Sarah.

She wrinkled her nose.

More of a reflexive action, I hoped, rather than because of any smell.

Her face relaxed and she smiled. "Oh, I knew you'd find a way to take his mind off his troubles."

I flushed, quite sure I was a deep scarlet. For all my years of being naked on screen, I still tended to keep my sex life private.

She raised her hand to caress my cheek. "From the moment I met you, I knew you'd heal him. You'd love him. You'd protect him. Glad you haven't disappointed me."

Her words meant everything. I didn't need her approval, of course, but having it eased a tightness in my chest. I wanted this family to embrace me as one of their own—and they had.

"I was just heading to bed." She tapped the large headphones resting around the base of her neck. "Make as much noise as you want." With that, she spun, and sauntered back toward her room.

Okay, then.

The lights in the bathroom were bright, and I wet a washcloth with warm water then ran it over my chest, belly, cock, and balls. There were times I couldn't believe how much cum Thomas had in him.

Tossing that cloth in the hamper, I wet another one with scalding water and headed back to our room.

Thomas hadn't moved.

The light from the lamp cast a warm glow in the room. His skin, normally so pale, was darker. He wasn't buff and muscular like me, but that was just fine. He was fine. Lean and supple. Strong and defiant, yet soft and gentle. He was a bundle of contradictions. That's what attracted me the most to him.

"Are you going to ogle me all day or are you going to wash me?" There was a note of petulance in his voice, but he was teasing.

"It's a sight I'll never tire of." I moved to his side of the bed, sitting so our thighs touched. Slowly, with deliberate care, I washed him. First his cock and balls, then moving on to his belly and chest. Finally, I took his right hand and scrubbed it clean as well. I believed in being thorough.

He moaned in pleasure and laid his left hand against my forearm. "I love when you take care of me."

I managed to push, "I love taking care of you," past the lump in my throat. I rose and he scooted over while I removed the towel and replaced it with the clean one that had been around my waist. He arched his eyebrow.

"I'm hedging my bets." There were nights when we'd go at it all night and just as often nights when we slept soundly. I couldn't predict which kind of night this one would be.

He snagged the sheet and covers, holding them up in invitation.

No further encouragement needed. I scooted in, prepared to pull him into an embrace.

"You lie on your side. I want to spoon you."

Okay.

Not what I'd expected. But then when had Thomas ever been predictable? I shifted, and he pulled the blankets over us and then drew me into a tight embrace. His now-cool chest pressed against my back. His groin cradled my ass as his thighs pressed to mine. He tucked his arm under mine, laying his hand flat against my chest, right above my heart. His hand was chilly, but the rest of him wasn't and he was soon warming me up.

He pressed a kiss to my shoulder blade, nipped the skin, then soothed the love bites with his tongue. Again, not what I'd expected. This was something he did when he was frisky and wanting to play. I didn't foresee we were going that way.

"I'm marking you," he said in answer to my unasked question. "Letting the world know you're mine."

Despite myself, I laughed. "No one is going to see that bite." And he hadn't done it hard enough to leave a sting, let alone a mark.

"Well, you'll know."

"I've always been yours, Thomas, and I always will be."

If possible, his grip tightened even further.

I rested my hand over his, stroking my fingers over his knuckles. Although he was easy to rile, he was just as easy to soothe. I wanted to tell him how brave he'd been tonight. How proud I was of him. How he never had to fear his parents' disapproval. But the words wouldn't come. Couldn't come. To say them now, in this quiet space, might disrupt the peace that'd settled over us, embracing us in a cocoon. Time enough for talk tomorrow.

Chapter Five

Thomas

I slid two fingers into Peter's hole with relative ease.

He shifted, slowly pulling from sleep to wakefulness.

"I'd ask what time it is, but that doesn't really matter." His voice was sleep-laden, husky, and sexy as fuck.

My balls, already quite heavy, grew heavier. My already hard cock, hardened further. I twisted my wrist and hit his prostate. He gasped and clenched around my fingers.

"Jesus, Thomas, do that again."

I loved it when he begged. Or ordered. Or did just about anything.

"Roll onto your belly and stick your ass in the air. I'm going to pound your tight ass."

It took mere moments for him to comply. I rarely topped since I derived so much pleasure from having him in me. Having him dominate him. Having him love me. However, when the mood struck me, I could be as aggressive and dominant as he was. He'd submit and later admit he enjoyed a good pounding now and again. We rarely negotiated these things. We didn't need to. If he ever said *no,* then of course I'd stop.

He'd never said *no.*

Rolling onto his belly, he tucked his legs up his chest and stuck his ass in the air. Panting, he pulled his cheeks apart, giving me the most gorgeous view. I'd slicked up my cock and now it was just a matter of lining myself up and pressing home. I did, but slowly. Inch by inch I entered him, feeling him grip me. The embrace was intimate, and I was glad we'd ditched condoms as soon as we'd committed. Which was, like, ten minutes after the first time we'd made love. He was my first. My true first. That guy, from high school, he didn't count.

Jesus, *not* the time to be thinking of him.

Focus.

"You said you were going to pound me."

Peter's way of refocusing me. I pushed all the way in so my groin slapped his ass.

He groaned.

Then I pounded him. Fucked him right into the mattress. My thrusts were rough as my fingers gripped his hips. I barely gave him room to catch his breath before I'd go at it again. My own breath was coming in quick gasps. Not long. Not...

"Jerk yourself." Normally I liked to do it for him, but tonight was not the night for that. I needed him to orgasm so I could go over the precipice as well.

His jerks were brutal, his breathing harsh.

Not long— His shout of release was all the permission I needed. Even as he tightened around me, I let go and was coming. But I heard...music?

Was that, like, angels singing? Some monumental spiritual moment?

"Your phone," Peter rasped. "Hailey's ringtone."

Oh shit. Oh shit. Oh shit.

I yanked out of him and he yelped, but I couldn't pause to take care of him. Hailey never called. It wasn't her jam. She would give us a time and we would call her. We were due to call her tomorrow afternoon. No, no, no...

I snatched the phone and swiped before it could go to voicemail. "Hailey? What's wrong?"

"I'm in the hospital." Her voice was small and tentative.

My heart sank. I almost dropped the phone before I put it on speaker phone so Peter could hear.

He collected himself first. "What's going on, Hailey? What did the doctor say?"

"Something about blood pressure and that was why I was so dizzy. I almost passed out when I went to the store, and some nice guy called an ambulance, and now they're saying I have to stay, and I'm so *scared*."

I glanced at the bedside table. Barely eleven. Felt like a million years since dinner but it'd merely been five hours. So much had happened since then.

"Hailey, can you put the doctor on the phone? Or a nurse?" Peter was calm.

Far calmer than I was.

"I'm alone." Her voice was barely above a whisper. "Can you come?"

"Of course. Thomas and I will be there as soon as we can. But we're out of town, remember? We have a long way to come, but we'll get there as soon as we can." Peter pointed to his phone and mouthed *text Trinity*.

Right. Hailey's case worker. She'd know what to do, right? I removed the phone from the charger and fumbled several times as I struggled to compose a message that seemed coherent. I pressed Send.

Peter was still speaking softly to Hailey. Telling her everything was going to be okay and that we'd be there soon.

But would we?

He said to trust the doctors and nurses to take care of her.

But would they?

I rolled off the bed and grabbed the still damp washcloth and tried to wash the lube and cum off my cock. Yeah, not how I'd envisioned tonight going. I sorted through our discarded clothes until I found my briefs, socks, jeans, and a shirt.

Success.

Even my sweater was easy to find. I was organizing Peter's clothes when his phone rang. Trinity. I answered, leaving the room to go stand in the hall.

"I got your message, Peter. What's going on?"

"This is Thomas. Peter's on my phone talking to Hailey. She said she almost passed out in a store, and they took her by ambulance to the hospital, and now the doctors want her to stay. Something about her blood pressure being high. Is any of this making sense?"

"It does." Something rustled. "Can you find out if they took her to VGH?"

"Sure." I poked my head back in the room and gestured at Peter. "Is she at Vancouver General?"

"No, B.C. Women's Hospital," came the quiet response from the phone.

I'd forgotten she was on speaker. I stepped back into the hall. "B.C. Women's Hospital."

"Okay." More rustling. "I'm in Mission City, and that's more than an hour away, plus there's a massive rainstorm. I'll call the hospital to see what the doctor says. If they'll let me, I'll go and sit with her." Even more rustling. "Where are you guys?"

"Prince George. We're visiting my parents over Christmas. We thought we had two months, or we would never have left town."

"It sounds like you may still have time. You need to stay calm, Thomas. How's the weather your way?"

"Massive snowstorm. I doubt we'll be able to get a pilot to fly in this weather."

Clicking noises. "Hmm, Prince George airport is closed and there are highway advisories all up and down the 97. Look, you take it easy. I'll get you some answers, and when the weather clears, you can decide if you need to come home, or if you can finish your stay with your parents."

"Make sure Hailey's okay. That's the most important thing."

A sigh. "Of course we know that, Thomas. I'll call as soon as I have news." With that, she disconnected.

My heart in my throat and my stomach clenched, I headed back into my bedroom.

Peter was dressing and my phone lay on the bed.

"And?"

"She said she was tired and wanted to rest. She apologized for calling and I kept telling her she'd done the right thing." He pointed to his phone. "What did Trinity say?"

"She'll call the doctor and see if she can get an update. Apparently, the PG airport is closed, and there are highway advisories everywhere."

He dropped to the bed, his jeans still undone and his shirt open.

I didn't remember ever seeing him so dejected. I crouched down between his legs, looking up into his stormy green eyes.

"Trinity is there. Well, close by, anyway. Trinity will take care of her until we can get to her."

He swallowed audibly. "I feel like we were wrong to come up here. We should have stayed closer."

I cupped his cheek. "The doctor told us it would be fine. We hired people to go in and take care of her."

"Then why did she go to the store?"

"Because she's nineteen and wants to be independent. You know she hates being cooped up in her apartment."

"She should be staying with us."

We'd had that argument dozens of times with Hailey, but she'd been adamant. Yes, she was willing to give us her baby. No, she wasn't willing to impose on us before the baby was born. As if having her there so we could care for her was an imposition.

Trinity had explained Hailey was told she was an imposition almost her entire life and had internalized that. She was old enough to recognize she wasn't mature enough and secure enough to keep her baby, but her emotional growth was stunted. Nothing Peter or I said or did made any difference.

And she could change her mind at any time. Peter and I would support her no matter her decision, but keeping the baby really wasn't viable for her. She had enough shit to deal with, including an addiction that was always there, lurking just below the surface. She wasn't using because of the baby, but we all knew she'd be back on the streets as soon as she could if she didn't get the help she needed.

"We need to get to Vancouver." Peter's eyes were full of desperation.

"I get that." Look at me being all calm and rational.

"Well, we can't grow wings and fly." His voice rose.

"Not in a snowstorm, no. Flying is definitely out." I kept my tone level.

A small smile crept on his face. "I hate it when you're logical."

Which made two of us. We were both rational and logical men who believed in the power of love. That optimism had helped us find a social worker who worked with unwed pregnant teen mothers. In turn, she'd matched us with a girl willing to give her baby up for adoption to two men. Peter's celebrity status had held zero sway—she hadn't even known who he was.

We'd contemplated surrogacy but had decided this was a better route to try. We hadn't ruled out adopting older children, either. For sure, we were united in our desire to be parents.

"You said there's an advisory on the highway. Does that mean no traffic is getting through?"

Something I should have thought to verify. "I'll check while you finish getting dressed." Not that I didn't love him disheveled, but that wouldn't get us closer to our goal.

I was studying the phone trying to decide what to check or who to call when there was a knock at the door.

Sarah stood there in her flannel onesie looking adorable with pigtails and a sleepy expression. "Not that it's any of my business, but what's going on? You sounded panicked."

"Weren't you wearing headphones?" Oh God, had she heard me when I was pounding Peter into the mattress? His moans? My cries? Sweet Jesus.

She rolled her eyes. "I was heading to the bathroom." Said headphones were in her hands. "I so do not want to know what you were doing before, but I can see something's happened. Can I help?"

"Only if you know a way to get us magically to Vancouver in the next, oh, few hours."

She wrinkled her nose.

God, I hoped she couldn't smell the sex.

"Let me ask Dad."

Peter finally rose from the bed. "We don't want to involve your parents, Sarah. It's nice of you to offer to help, but this is our problem."

She waggled her finger at him. "You're family, so this is now a family problem. Dad and Mom'll be pissed if you don't tell them what's going on."

She wasn't wrong.

I exchanged a long look with Peter. We'd decided to not tell anyone about Hailey. She had the right to change her mind at any time, and until we had the baby safely in our custody, we weren't going to tell anyone. We didn't want to jinx it.

But this was my family, and I was tired of keeping secrets from them.

"Yeah, Sarah, go wake them up. Maybe we can solve this problem if we all put our heads together."

In a flash she was gone. Peter glanced down at his bare chest, grimaced, and did up the buttons.

"She's seen it all before." I wasn't referring just to the on-screen stuff. We'd hung out around the pool when the family had come down for Labor Day. I distinctly remember we three men being shirtless. Dad's less-than-perfect body, and his comfort with it, had eased my stress about going topless. Sarah had worn a ridiculously tiny bikini, and Mom had refused to change out of her sundress. What a perfect afternoon.

Peter put on his socks while I checked the radar. Yep, plenty of color across most of British Columbia. Green down in Vancouver and white up here in PG. Didn't look like there was any sleet or freezing rain between here and there, but conditions could turn on a dime this time of year.

My husband tossed clothes into our suitcases haphazardly, which was so not like him. He was almost as neat and meticulous as I was. Yet another thing I loved about him.

"We put all the gifts for your family under the tree, right? And they're all labeled?"

"Yes." I snagged the bottle of lube.

He'd just tucked it under pajama bottoms when Mom called from down the hall.

"We'll be right down." I didn't want her to come in while we were still in such disarray.

"Okay, dear."

Sarah reappeared. "They were still awake, so no biggie."

Except it was, and we both knew it. My parents were early-to-bed, early-to-rise people. Their bedtime was just short of ten. For them to be awake past eleven was something of note. I just didn't have time to do more than note it.

Peter handed me one suitcase and had the other. "If we've forgotten anything, we can have them ship it to us. Or we can come back to get it."

Or we could just buy it new. There wasn't anything that couldn't be replaced. I leaned in to give him a long kiss. Yes, it ate up valuable time, but he needed to be reminded we were in this together. That he wasn't alone. That he'd never be alone again.

And maybe I also needed the reminding.

The suitcases were lighter since we'd unloaded the gifts under the tree. There weren't a lot of them, and I hadn't let my husband go over the top spending lots of money because it'd only embarrass my parents. They owned their house, had good retirement packages, and lived comfortably. They didn't need—nor would they want—to be lavished with unnecessary gifts. But now that Dad was retiring, that travel voucher would hopefully get used.

Mom sat at the kitchen table in her chenille bathrobe and Dad wore his terry towel one, belted low at the waist. They looked amazingly awake for the hour. Mom had turned on the coffee maker, and I hoped they weren't planning to indulge. They needed sleep. Peter and I had enjoyed about two hours of it and that was enough to feel refreshed. Or we were running on adrenaline. Hard to say.

Dad was pacing, but he stopped when we entered the room. "Get to it, young man. What is going on and how can we help?"

"Yes," Mom added quickly. "Sit, please. I don't need anyone else pacing."

My father gave her a pointed look but did sit. Peter and I did the same and Sarah plopped down in her seat. The headphones were gone, and she tilted her head in interest.

Peter took my hand and we rested our joined ones on the top of the table. I swear Mom's gaze softened. How often had I worried about her approval? I sure didn't anymore.

"Thomas and I..." He cleared his throat. "Thomas and I decided early on that we wanted to raise a family. Be parents." He pointedly looked at both my parents. "He and I both had excellent role models, and we hoped if we could be half the parents you and my family were, we'd do okay."

Mom pressed a hand to her heart and this time, her eyes shimmered.

I took up the story. "We started asking around, and a social worker introduced us to a program where pregnant women find families for their babies. They give up custody but have the choice to stay in touch if they chose. Like an open adoption. I don't know how it happened, but we sailed through the approval process, and they matched us with a young woman. They told us it could be years, and we'd already begun the process of becoming foster parents. Times have changed, to be sure, but gay couples still face hurdles."

"Hailey chose us." Peter squeezed my hand. "She swore she didn't know who I was. She just liked that we could provide for her child. That her child would never live in poverty or know financial deprivation. Also, she, I think, saw the love Thomas and I have for each other and knew we would share that love with a child."

I took up the harder part of the story. "Hailey was using when she got pregnant and she was at the end of her first trimester before she even realized she was expecting. She's on methadone to curb the addiction, but it's pretty much guaranteed the baby's going to be born with an opioid addiction. She's facing a lifetime of challenges."

"She?" Dad's voice was barely above a whisper. "We're going to have a granddaughter?" Now his eyes shimmered too.

"We're still far from that," Peter said. "And here's where we need help. Hailey is in the hospital and asking for us. She's scared, and although her case worker is trying to get there as soon as she can, Hailey's made it clear she wants Thomas and me to be there. For whatever happens."

"And you don't know what's happening?" Sarah yanked at one of her pigtails. Hard. Something she did during times of stress.

I wanted to reassure her but, hell, I needed reassurance myself.

"Trinity, her case worker, will call as soon as she has news. Until then, we just have to get to Vancouver as soon as we can."

My mother glanced at the window. She couldn't see out, but her unspoken concern was written all over her face.

"They're predicting snow for another day or two, and then it'll take them time to clear the runways and resume operations." Information I'd gleaned from the weather site.

Dad strode over to the phone and started looking through the old-fashioned cloth-covered personalized address book that Mom'd owned, I could swear, for her entire marriage. Picking up the phone, he dialed.

Peter and I exchanged what felt like the millionth glance before looking at Mom who just shrugged.

"Ralph? It's Bart Walsh. Sorry to wake you." Pause. "Oh, well, glad you're awake. You on shift?" Another pause. "I figured with the storm you might be up. Look, I need a favor. I won't say I'm calling one in because friends and neighbors help each other out, and of course, we'll always be here if you or Marg need something."

Another pause.

"Right, well, my boy and his husband need to get to Vancouver. It's an emergency. A big one. I know you can't get them that far, but could you do Williams Lake? Maybe Cache Creek?"

Another nerve-shattering pause. This one went on forever.

"Oh, I see." Dad rubbed his hand across his face. "That would be..." He swallowed audibly. "And you think...?" His voice broke. "Yeah, they're ready to go right now."

I squeezed Peter's hand. I didn't want to get my hopes up, and I didn't even know who Ralph was. But I'd owe him forever if he could get us closer to Vancouver. Closer to Hailey. Closer to home.

"Fifteen minutes." Dad smiled. "Yeah, and I'll owe you big time." He hung up.

"Ralph is sending a Hydro Truck. They need to check out some lines close to Williams Lake and, of course, they'll need to stop there before coming back. Now, Ralph used to run crews out of Cache Creek, and he figures he can get one of his guys to do a run between Williams Lake, through Cache Creek and on maybe as far as Hope. That'll get you to the TransCanada, and as long as it's open, you should be able to catch some kind of lift to Vancouver."

Oh. My. God. Had Dad just arranged everything? In one phone call? I released Peter's hand, leapt to my feet, took the two steps, and embraced my dad. Squeezing, I pulled him in for a bear hug like the ones he used to give me when I was a kid and in need of support. The one guaranteed to bring comfort.

"Well, you boys will need coffee for the road." Mom rose and moved to the cupboards. Dad rubbed my head the way he used to. Only now I didn't have long hair to muss.

I wouldn't have cared even if I had.

"Do you have enough mugs to give us a couple?" Peter being Peter, of course.

My mother opened the cabinet to reveal at least five. "People keep giving them to your dad. I think I have four more downstairs in a box." She winked. "And I suspect you'll send us replacement ones anyway."

She knew my husband.

Pulling down the two insulated cups, she set about making the coffees—exactly the way we took them. Observant, as usual. Mine was almost half cream with heaps of sugar. No Starbucks open around here where I could get a latté and no time to stop anywhere else. Peter preferred his black on a night like this. She also removed an insulated lunch bag from the fridge and started filling it with food. "Do I have time to make roast beef sandwiches?"

Dad glanced at his watch. "If you make it quick. You boys better, well, you know."

Take a piss? "Yeah, Dad, we know. I'll go upstairs and Peter can use the bathroom down here."

We took off in our separate directions as Mom removed the mustard from the fridge. Yep, she knew us.

I was quick and took a moment to splash cold water on my face. Refreshing and invigorating. I'd need it in this weather. For this journey. For this night. I was halfway down the stairs when Peter's phone rang as he was coming out of the bathroom.

He mouthed *Trinity* before swiping.

"I have good news and not-so-good news."

I liked her no-nonsense approach to the situation.

"Go ahead." Peter's voice was steady, but his hand wasn't.

"Hailey is stable. They've got her blood pressure down and she's resting comfortably."

"What's the not-so-good news?"

"The doctor is worried about pre-eclampsia. She wants to keep the baby in as long as possible, of course, but she's worried that if they can't control Hailey's blood pressure... things could go badly for both of them. They're keeping her here for a day or two but if she's released, it'll be under strict bed-rest orders."

"She'll come home with us." Peter was firm. "We've given her leeway and respected her wishes, but her life is as important as the baby's. We'd never be able to live with ourselves if something happened to either of them and we could've prevented it."

I pressed my hand to his arm and leaned toward the speaker. "Or we can get her round-the-clock nursing care if she insists on staying in her apartment. I mean, we should probably do that anyway." My husband had been insisting for six months that I accept it was *our* money. Well, now was as a good time as any to make that change in mindset.

Trinity let out a breath. "Yeah, I figured I could count on you guys. You know—"

"She might change her mind." Peter blinked his sea-green eyes several times. "We've always accepted that, Trinity. Just...make sure she's okay. Whatever you need to do."

"Already on it." A car door slammed. "I'm heading to Vancouver now, but it's going to be a slow slog. There's already flooding in some areas. If you guys make it down, be careful, eh?"

Peter's eyes crinkled in amusement. They always did when he heard the Canadian expression.

"We will, Trinity." I tentatively smiled, and tried to inject optimism into my next words. "It looks like we've got a ride heading south. It's going to take us a long time, but we'll get there."

"Thomas, you and Peter are two of the most determined men I've ever met. Just be safe, okay?"

"We will. Thank you."

My husband's words were soft and heartfelt.

"Gotta run." The line went dead.

The doorbell rang.

I held on to Peter's arm for just one moment longer before releasing it and heading for the door.

A short stout woman stood at the door, brushing the snow off her uniform jacket. "You Thomas and Peter?"

"We are."

"Well, let's get going. I heard the plow's hitting the highway in about ten minutes and I aim to be the first vehicle behind him."

Understanding her meaning, I turned to head to the kitchen, but my family appeared.

Mom carried the mugs, Sarah had the insulated bag slung over her shoulder, and my father had a stern expression and our two suitcases.

I wanted to protest, but that'd be rude. He was a healthy man in his late fifties. He could carry a couple of suitcases.

Peter opened the hall closet door and we began the arduous task of layering our clothes.

"I like to keep my truck on the cool side," the woman said. "Bring all your winter gear in case something happens. Be prepared and all that shit." She flushed and glanced at my mother. "Apologies, ma'am."

"Not anything I haven't heard before." Mom's smile was tight. "You'll take care of them?"

"Yes, ma'am. I been doing this run for about fifteen years. I know my way around electricity and snow. Hope I only see snow tonight." She glanced behind her. "But with how heavy and thick the snow is, I suspect at least one line or two'll go down."

After I finished lacing my second boot, I held out my hand. "I'm Thomas and this is my husband Peter."

Peter finished lacing his boot at that moment and glanced up to meet the woman's appraising gaze.

"Name's Gisele. Say your goodbyes and I'll meet you at the truck."

Before I could say anything, she yanked the suitcases from my dad's grasp and was pushing her way out the door.

Well, okay then.

Sarah grabbed me by the neck and enfolded me in a massive hug. I easily engulfed her tiny frame with my one-foot height advantage. Peter embraced Mom and received the obligatory kiss to his cheek. He moved on to Dad and I stepped toward my mother. She placed both her hands on my cheek and I had to stoop for her. Where Sarah was svelte, our mother had a few extra pounds. Yet she carried herself with grace and dignity. I could only hope to be so happy when I reached her age. Her hug was just as tight and my eyes watered. I'd lost ten years because of my irrational belief that I'd caused Luke's death. Thanks to Peter's encouragement, I'd reconnected with my roots.

My hug with Dad was shorter. We'd had our moment in the kitchen. With waves and best wishes, Peter and I stepped out into the storm. We could barely see the white truck with its ladder and bucket on the roof. The vehicle would be sturdy, for sure, but I was still nervous. I used to be cavalier about my own safety, but I'd become more cautious in the last six months. I had something to live for. I had someone who counted on me.

I squinted as we neared the truck. That was going to fit three of us? And where had Gisele stored the luggage?

She opened the door and pointed to me. "Skinnier boy gets the middle seat. Strap in, boys." Without further ado, she went around to the driver's side and hauled herself up.

Seeing no alternative, I hoisted myself up and placed the cooler bag in the footwell. I quickly secured my seat belt and took the coffee mugs from Peter so he could get in as well. Only as he did up his belt did I appreciate how windy it'd been. The wind still whipped the snow sideways, and I had flakes on my eyelashes.

Gisele was strapped in. She hadn't turned the truck off, so all she had to do was put it in gear and we were off.

I glanced back at my childhood home, but the lights were barely visible, let alone shadows of my family. I could only hope they'd be safe and warm and able to fall asleep.

A few turns took us out of the neighborhood, and soon we were on the highway. The road appeared plowed, and I finally breathed a sigh of relief.

"They only sand the turns, so it's still icy." Gisele said these words as if they were of no consequence. "But you guys are belted in tight. I been doing this for twenty years and never had a crash."

Somewhat reassuring.

"You've driven wayward strangers to Williams Lake in the middle of snowstorms for twenty years?"

I couldn't believe Peter was making a joke, but the set of his jaw betrayed how stressed he was. I pressed our shoulders together and took his hand in mine. I'd have preferred skin-to-skin contact, but the freezing temperature in the cab precluded that.

Gisele chortled. "Nope, this is a first. But Ralph's a great guy. He gave me my first line job when not many women were doing the work. He's made sure the guys knew he expected them to treat me with respect and take me seriously. That doesn't always happen. So, yeah, he calls in a favor and I'm happy to do it."

I tried to focus on her words and not the fact I couldn't see ten feet beyond the windshield.

"Your dad's a good man. He was there for Ralph's family when they needed support. I'm not surprised Ralph's returning the favor."

Okay, with an opening like that, how was I not supposed to jump through? "Yeah, Dad's a good guy." A lump caught in my throat. "The best."

Gisele nodded. "He is that. Ralph's son nearly died in a wreck on the highway about five years back. It looked bad for a while. But your dad was right there, offering comfort. We all knew his son—your brother—had died in similar circumstances, so that he stepped up was amazing. Ralph's kid is in a wheelchair, but he's alive. Just finished a degree in counseling. Ralph'll swear that was your dad's doing."

And yet I knew none of this. Ralph's son was, by my calculation, around Sarah's age. And since I hadn't kept up with what was going on in PG, how would I have ever known? And the fact Dad had undoubtedly relived the pain he'd endured after Luke's death? Again, it spoke to the amazing man he was. The amazing man I hadn't given enough credit to. I'd hidden my sexuality because I worried he'd judge me harshly. Instead he'd been hurt I hadn't confided in him earlier.

Peter squeezed my hand, pulling me from my reverie. He nudged me with his shoulder. "I'm sorry?"

Gisele laughed. "I was saying my daughter was just a couple of years behind Sarah."

I did a double take. Gisele couldn't have been over thirty-five. But then she said she'd been doing this for twenty years.

"I was nineteen when I had my baby. I came to Hydro two years later. Earned my stripes while my mom babysat. I was one of the lucky ones. Could have wound up on welfare. Stupid to get pregnant that young. But I can't regret my baby girl who is definitely not a baby." She laughed softly. "Calls herself pansexual. Has brought home boys and girls. I don't give a crap as long as they treat her right."

Oh, okay.

"So what I'm saying is you two being together doesn't bother me. Gives me hope my girl will meet the right person. I'd just be happy if she waited a dozen years before settling down."

"Twenty-eight is a good age."

Peter snickered.

"Okay, so is forty-two."

Gisele chanced a brief look at Peter. "You do *not* look that old."

"Moisturizer and staying out of the sun whenever possible."

I snickered. "Texas via LA doesn't give you much chance to stay out of the sun."

"I do my best."

He did. He was a stickler for sunscreen. Didn't want to lose another partner to cancer. Not that Desmond had ever been a partner to him in the true sense. Not like we were. And that thought brought me comfort. I planned to have the next fifty or so years together.

Gisele slammed on the brakes.

Oh, taillights. Instinctively I reached out to hold Peter back as he did the same for me. We strained against our safety belts and I waited for the inevitable crash. My mind flashed to Luke. Was this the panic he must have felt the split second before the crash? Before he died? Or had it happened so fast he didn't realize? I'd always taken comfort in knowing he'd died on impact. No suffering.

The crunch never came. Gisele moved us across the center line. A gamble, to be sure, but there was no shoulder in this stretch and likely not much oncoming traffic. Once we stopped, she asked, "you guys okay?"

I wanted to make a remark about having ten years shaved off my life, but Peter answered.

"We're fine. What do you need us to do?"

She cocked her head as if making mental calculations. We had to get out of this lane, that much was clear. Deciding, she pulled past the car and then pulled back into our lane. She shoved her hat on her head, hiding her riot of curls. She unlatched her safety belt, donned her gloves, and hopped down out of the truck.

Were we supposed to follow? Stay where we were?

"They might need our help." Peter's voice was tight.

"If they do, Gisele will tell us, I'm sure."

He yanked off his glove to check his phone. "It's already two-thirty. How far to Williams Lake?"

I had a vague notion of where we were, which wasn't far. "It's about two hundred and fifty kilometers. Two-and-a-half hours in good weather."

Peter huffed. "Can I get that in English?"

I muttered *Arrogant American* under my breath as I did the calculation. "One hundred and fifty-five miles. I'd say we've done about thirty." If that.

A bang had us both sitting up. "A door." He shoved his phone back into his pocket and put his glove back on. "That was just a door."

Of course it was. A crash would've been a lot louder.

Before we could say more, Gisele was back. She hauled herself into the cab, removed her hat and gloves, and put the truck back in gear.

What...?

She picked up the radio and rattled off a bunch of information that made little sense to me. I caught mile something, that there was a broken-down car, and that she'd laid flares to warn anyone coming.

Dispatch responded that they'd alerted RCMP who were also likely to call a tow truck.

"What a mess," she huffed. "Stupid idiot shouldn't have been driving in this. He went into a skid, hit the snowbank, and now he's stuck. But he's got plenty of fuel, so he can run the car to heat it up once in a while. He'll be fine as long as no one rear-ends him. Tail pipe is clear so he shouldn't get carbon monoxide poisoning."

Like we almost had.

And we were off again. This time we were going slower, and although it ratcheted up my stress about Hailey, it lowered my concern about being in a crash. About twenty minutes later, taillights were visible again.

"Hot damn, that's the snowplow."

I appreciated Gisele's enthusiasm. The snowplow would be slow us down, but it'd also make things much safer for us. Only another few minutes passed before Peter rested his head on my shoulder. His breathing evened out.

How could he sleep? I mean, I was tired, but also filled with adrenaline. I eased his coffee mug from his hand. I would've drunk it, but needing to pee in the middle of nowhere was not my idea of fun. Leaning back, I settled in for the ride.

Chapter Six

Peter

A light kiss to my temple and Thomas' softly uttered, "wake up," pulled me into awareness. Within a fraction of a second, I was fully alert. "Where are we?"

"Williams Lake." He pointed out the window. "Tim Horton's. We make a pit stop and then we get into another Hydro truck."

We were going to owe favors to everyone from Prince George to Vancouver.

"Did your dad help this person as well?"

Thomas smiled. "Nope. Just a good Samaritan who loves company. He'll take us to Cache Creek." He nudged me. "I've got to go because I drank my entire coffee."

Darkness still shrouded the world, broken by the bright-pink fluorescent lights of the parking lot. Snow still fell, but not sideways anymore.

"The wind?" I unclipped my safety belt and opened the door. Within moments, I had the answer to my question. Calm enveloped me along with the falling snow. Once Thomas was beside me, we hurried into Timmie's. Never had I been so grateful for this great Canadian staple. I made a beeline for the nearest restroom, did my business quickly, and came out. Damn, should have let Thomas go first. He was, after all, the one who'd drunk all his coffee.

"You get fresh coffees while I freshen up." His eyes were dull in the store's light.

"You want something to eat?"

"We've got Mom's sandwiches, but I wouldn't say no to a maple donut."

At least his taste in donuts was a little saner than his taste in ice cream. Tiger tail. I still laughed at my initial reaction to the orange cream and black licorice.

I looked around for Gisele so I could order something for her as well, but she was nowhere to be found.

The young woman behind the counter wore a hijab and a huge smile. A little too bright for... Oh, hell, what difference did the time make?

I handed her the mugs. "Could you rinse them out? Then one latte and one Double Double." Not my favorite, but a little sugar and milk never hurt anyone. "Oh, and one maple dip and one vanilla with sprinkles." Yeah, I loved my sprinkles. She rang in the order and I tapped my card then dropped five toonies in the tip jar. Her eyes widened. "You're working. I'm appreciative."

Her eyes narrowed, and for a moment I wondered if she recognized me. Instead she gave a nod of thanks and took our mugs over to the sink. By the time she handed me the coffees and donuts, Gisele had reappeared.

"Clive'll take you as far as Cache Creek. We're still trying to work out how to get you to Hope. In Hope you're going to have to find your own way. But you'll be at the TransCanada so I'm sure you'll find someone there. Maybe even a bus, if they're still running."

I pulled out my wallet and started counting bills. My tendency to carry a lot of cash drove Thomas nuts, but today it was a good habit to have.

Gisele scowled. "What the fuck you think you're doing?"

Stunned, I stilled my hands. She hadn't cursed when it looked like we were going to crash but was doing it now? "Paying you." Wasn't this obvious?

Her scowl deepened.

I hadn't thought that possible, but it was.

"Put your money away. It means nothing up here in these parts. We're all neighbors, and we watch out for each other. You get my meaning?"

"I'll take his money."

"You do and I might kick you in the balls."

The new arrival to our little group laughed. He also wore a uniform jacket. "I'm kidding, Gisele." He pointed to her. "She's got no sense of humor."

She glared.

I tucked my wallet away. We could settle up at Cache Creek. Thomas came up behind me and took the mug from my hand. I handed him the paper bag with his donut.

"Well, Gisele, we really appreciate what you've done for us."

She shot one more glare at Clive. "He'll take good care of you."

Clive gave her a pat on the back that was none too light. "You're a good woman."

"And I'm still not marrying you."

Ah, that explained a lot.

Gisele waved and headed off toward the washrooms.

"Common guys, don't want to waste any more time."

We followed Clive out to his truck and repeated the process—Thomas in the middle, me next to the window. Apparently, Gisele had handed over our suitcases and cooler bag while we'd dithered in the store. Within moments we were on our way. I'd barely taken my first sip when Clive spoke.

"So y'all are married, right? I didn't support that gay marriage thing at first but my mother was all, like, you can't choose who you love and I was like, aw Mom, I don't want to think about two guys having sex and she was like, it's not just about sex and...well, she plum wore me down. Now I figure, you know, live and let live."

"That's a very enlightened attitude." Was that the right thing to say? I certainly didn't want to offend him.

"I know, right?" He pulled back onto the highway. "'Cause I'm an enlightened guy."

And he continued on. And on.

I don't think he drew breath the entire four-hour trip. A trip that normally took two-and-a-half, mind. Thomas nodded off just before 100 Mile House and I envied him. I made the occasional grunt of agreement, or noise of approval but, frankly, I didn't think Clive noticed. Did he speak to himself when he was alone, driving up and down these desolate roads?

There wasn't a Tim Horton's in Cache Creek—much to my surprise. I thought every town had the ubiquitous icons. There was an

A&W in the Chevron gas station, so that was good enough. I raced to the washroom ahead of Thomas, who was still groggy from his four-hour nap. Lucky bastard slept through the entire trip.

I emerged to find Clive frowning. My heart sank.

"Earl got called in because there's a downed line. Dispatch was thrilled I was here to help, although a little curious why I was so far south. I made up some bullshit story. Anyway, I'm sorry I couldn't help more. But hey, the Number One—the TransCanada—meets the 97 here in town. I suggest hanging out in the truck park until you find someone. I checked and the bus isn't running."

So, no magical bus ride. I held back the weary sigh. "You were awesome, Clive." I pulled out my billfold.

He pocketed the five one-hundred-dollar bills I handed him. "Mom's in a nursing home."

"You don't need to explain."

"Yeah, but I don't want Gisele to know."

"My lips are sealed."

He saluted and was gone.

Thomas came up behind me. "Where's Earl?"

"They called Earl out because there's a downed power line."

He swore.

"Clive said something about trying out the truck stop. Would that be here or..."

Thomas shook his head. "There's a Husky down the road just after the Number One connects. That's where the truckers will be. It's less than a mile."

We both looked out the window. Daylight was finally upon us and the snow seemed to have lessened.

"You fellas need a lift?"

The tall young man with black eyeliner around his dark brown eyes couldn't have been over sixteen. His dark hair was pulled back into a ponytail.

"It's not legal to drive with two other people in the car when you've got your 'N'."

Thomas' expression was neutral, but I caught the desperation in his eyes. Sure we could walk, but in this snow? I doubted they plowed the sidewalks. If there were any.

"Robert."

The young man pivoted quickly and nearly tripped on a rack of chips. "Uh, hi Constable Singh, how are you?"

The RCMP officer didn't look impressed. He was also tall and lanky but had some serious heft to him. Gray was visible on his temples under his cap. His stone-faced look matched every officer of the Royal Canadian Mounted Police I'd ever met.

Not that I'd met many.

"Robert was just remembering that he can't carry two passengers with his 'N' license." The constable glared.

'N'...? Oh, New Driver. Yeah, no one under twenty-five either, but at least we didn't fit into that category.

"Uh, yeah, right." Robert ground his toe into a pile of slush. "But, like, they need a ride to the Husky."

Constable Singh gave us a once-over.

We stood there, clearly displaced persons. Our suitcases screamed expensive while we looked a little worse for wear. Almost ten hours on the road during a blizzard would do that to a person.

"I can give them a ride." The officer nodded to the young man. "You go on home. Stay out of trouble."

A flash of annoyance crossed Robert's face before he schooled his features. "Yes, sir." Within seconds, he was gone.

"What do you plan to do at the Husky?"

"Find a ride to Vancouver."

Thomas elbowed me in the gut.

"Hitchhiking is illegal." The constable didn't look impressed.

"Oh, we're not hitchhiking."

Thomas tossed me a *keep your mouth shut* look.

"We're hoping to hire a driver to take us down to Vancouver."

The officer looked dubious. After a moment, he relented. "Follow me. You'll have to sit in the back."

In one of my favorite movies, I'd been arrested and thrown into the back of a cop car. It'd been acting, but I'd felt oddly disconcerted. I wasn't looking forward to this at all. And Thomas had never been in the back of one either.

As far as I knew.

He picked up his suitcase with a determined look on his face. He had the cooler bag slung over one shoulder and his jaw looked like granite.

Yep, we were going to do this.

The snow had definitely lightened, and I could see farther down the street. Maybe this might work out. Was definitely worth a try. The officer opened the trunk, and we stowed our gear. He unlocked the door of the SUV and we piled in. We dutifully secured our seatbelts while he pulled out of the parking lot.

"Where were you gentlemen coming from?"

"PG," Thomas responded.

"And you didn't think to drive home?"

"We'd flown in two days ago. And there's an emergency in Vancouver that needs us, and the airport was closed, and the rental agencies were closed and..."

Heedless of the company, I grabbed his hand and held on. We needed to keep our shit together.

"And," the constable prodded.

"A few friends helped us get this far, but we're kind of stuck. We'd take a bus if we thought we could catch one."

Soon the Husky sign appeared. The constable flicked the turn signal and we entered the parking lot. He drove around back where a series of tractor trailers sat, neatly lined up.

Was he going to wait here with us? That seemed like a nice idea, but I didn't want to be imposing on the man. Or having him run interference. "We'll be on our way." I tried the door that was, of course, locked. "Uh, thank you so much for the ride."

He slid the SUV into a spot and got out. Soon he was unlocking Thomas' door and beckoning us out. Wordlessly, he pointed to the station and started walking.

We grabbed our suitcases from the trunk and followed.

The warm air was in stark contrast to the still-freezing temperatures outside.

A stunningly attractive woman stood behind the counter and waved when we walked in. She pointed to the back of the store. Constable Singh nodded and headed that way. We followed dutifully behind. At the door marked *Employees Only*, he knocked. About twenty seconds later a short woman answered the door. She was about Norma's height and I towered over her. All three of us had about a foot on her but she didn't look the least bit intimidated.

"What can I do for you?" She arched her brow.

He pointed to us. "These guys are looking for a ride to Vancouver. Or at least the Lower Mainland. Do you know anyone heading in that direction?"

She stuck a pen in her mouth and chewed on the end.

I almost gagged.

"Yeah, I know someone." She grabbed her coat off a hook and shoved her arms in as she hustled through the store. "But she might have already left." The woman was out the door in a flash and rounding the building.

She stuck her fingers in her mouth and whistled.

I thought my eardrums might burst.

The truck that had been pulling out ground to a halt. A moment later the cab opened, and the woman jumped down. "Good lord, Sharlene, what's the fuss about? I heard you over the music."

Sharlene waved her over.

"These two guys are looking for a ride to Vancouver. You're headed that way, right?"

The woman frowned. "I'm heading to Port Coquitlam. They can take the transit from there." She gave me and Thomas the once-over. "Yeah, they'll do. But they gotta come now. I'm already behind."

Constable Singh cleared his throat. "I have grave concerns about two men riding with you to Vancouver."

The woman blew a raspberry.

I yanked out my wallet. "You can take down all my information. And Thomas'." I nudged him and soon he was replicating my actions.

The cop did not look pleased.

"I see plenty of witnesses," the driver said. "You two get in the cab so we can go." She pointed to me. "I want you riding shotgun."

Okay. Whatever. Anything that kept us moving forward. The cop took our IDs and headed back toward his vehicle.

Oh. My. God.

"Look, I'm freezing." Sharlene headed back the way she came. To Thomas' *thank you* she waved her hand but didn't look back.

Had the snow lightened again? It still fell, but I could see the sign and the highway in the distance.

"Thomas, can you stow our bags?" His foot was tapping, so the time had come to give him a concrete task.

He grabbed the suitcases and nodded. "Uh, thank you ma'am."

"There's no *ma'am* around here. Name's Codi. With an 'i'. Get your butt in gear, kid. As soon as the cop's back, we're out of here."

My husband needed no further prompting. He went to the passenger door and hauled our suitcases up and then disappeared.

"We appreciate this." My wallet was in my hands and I mentally calculated how much we'd need. Transit fare in Vancouver was peanuts, and all done by electronics anyway, so our cards would take care. That meant I had—

"You wouldn't be thinking of paying me, would you?"

Damn perceptive woman. "Well..."

Her grin was downright wicked. "I get to tell everyone I had *the* Peter Erickson riding shotgun in my rig. That's better than any amount of money."

Well, there was that. I intended to leave a stash of cash in the glove compartment anyway.

With every second passing, more flakes of snow accumulated on my jacket. More time slipped away. More moments where Hailey was alone and scared in a hospital room. Neither of us had mentioned her. She still felt tenuous in our lives. Yes, she'd committed to us. Yes, she'd signed paperwork. But until we had our yet-unnamed daughter in our home, I didn't think I'd be able to draw a full breath.

"You okay?"

Codi's words broke through the fog. "Yeah, just...a little anxious to get back to Vancouver."

"You got some big movie or something?"

I shook my head. "No, something more personal."

"Fair enough."

Stomping my feet, I wondered about the temperature. And if we'd be lucky enough to get behind another snowplow. They were slow but made all the difference. Sensing eyes on me, I looked over to the truck where Thomas stared out the window. He held up his phone.

Fuck.

I was reaching into my pocket when Constable Singh exited his vehicle. He walked toward us with slow deliberate steps. Soon he was in front of us, but he made no move to return the IDs.

"You're American."

Could there *be* any more disdain? Possibly not.

"I am a permanent resident."

"Because you married."

Oh, okay. That game. "Yes, I married Thomas. We're in love. I also fell in love with Canada and that's where we've decided to make a home."

"But you could go back to the US."

Since America and Canada had a treaty, so could just about everyone else, unless they had a criminal record.

"I'm not a serial killer. I will not hurt Codi. I'm just a guy trying to get home."

"In a hurry." Still, he held those ID cards close to his chest. I wanted to rip them from him, jump in the cab, and drive away.

I didn't know how to drive an eighteen-wheeler, but I was willing to try.

Codi pointed at me. "This here is *the* Peter Erickson. You might not know who he is, but I do. And now you have his information. I need to get on the road."

"*The* Peter Erickson?" The note of disdain was clear. He glared down at Codi. "Doesn't mean they won't kill you. Or rape you. Or—"

Codi snatched the ID cards from his hand.

He appeared so startled, he let them go.

"You dumbass. They're gay. Don't mean they can't rape a woman, but it sure isn't their thing. This man is worth millions of dollars, so he isn't gonna risk losing all that. Not for little 'ole me."

Part of me wanted to argue that every woman had value and worth, but now was the moment, I believed, to keep my own counsel.

"Get in the truck, Peter." She handed me the driver's licenses as I passed. I hustled to the rig and hauled myself in. I barely had the door closed before Thomas had his arms around me from behind.

"I was so scared."

"I know." I had been as well but sharing that wouldn't ease his burden.

Codi was gesticulating wildly at the constable who looked less than impressed.

"Trinity called."

My heart sank.

"They're taking her for a C-section in an hour or so. They figure the baby will be born by two. She says the doctors are optimistic because she has made it to thirty-four weeks. The baby's lungs will be underdeveloped, and she'll be tiny, but they think..." His breath caught on a sob.

His pain ravaged me.

I gripped his hands that enveloped me. "It's out of our hands. She has the best medical care, and Trinity is with her. I'm sure everything will be fine." I wasn't a praying man, but I offered one in up that moment. For Hailey and for the baby. May they both be safe.

To my utter shock, Codi shook the constable's hand, then made her way over to us. I squeezed Thomas' hand one final time. "Strap in back there." He moved swiftly to do as bade, and I did the same.

Codi hauled herself into the rig, slammed the door, and let out a long breath.

I'd have sworn she muttered *asshole* under her breath, but I couldn't be sure and I sure as shit wasn't going to ask.

She put on her safety belt, put the truck in gear, and we were off.

The Constable still stood in the parking lot.

Codi saluted him and we drove away. As soon as she'd pulled out onto the highway, she turned on the radio and the opening bars of *Hamilton* filled the cab.

And then the snow stopped.

Chapter Seven

Thomas

Peter had introduced me to *Hamilton* when we first met. I'd heard of the musical, of course, but hadn't listened. The first ten times we listened he'd explained it slowly, character by character, plot line by plot line, political intrigue by historical context. I fell in love with the story. The story of someone who started from nothing and made a name for himself. I had a good solid middle-class upbringing, but when I moved to Vancouver, I had nothing. The life I now had was something I built. Something I could be proud of.

The show had been playing in LA, and Peter had flown me there for the weekend, not long after our wedding. We'd stayed in his home and, of course, I'd been in awe. A mansion barely described the enormous place. I didn't feel comfortable there, and Peter realized that pretty quickly. We watched the show and came back early.

And my husband assured me that our home in Shaughnessy was more than enough for him. Since it was one quarter the size of his American home, I did question that. When we shopped for a home, Peter wanted to look at big places, but I had balked. We settled on our home in a cozy family-friendly neighborhood. We could raise a family there.

A family that, if the fates aligned, would grow by one today.

Trinity's text had, of course, stressed me right the fuck out. I understood viability in a baby. God knows, Peter and I had read a massive pile of books about what to expect for both Hailey and our daughter. Hailey's life always came first—that was never up for debate. If we adopted a baby, that was a bonus. If the baby was born addicted to opioids, we would deal. There had been plenty of literature about that as well, and Trinity was a fount of knowledge.

This was the reason Peter was turning down the Yukon job. Managing a fragile infant would take all our time and effort. He accepted that. He said he'd be happy if he never worked again, but I didn't believe him. His talent left me in awe, and he had more to share with the world. He was ready to move from action hero to character roles with gravitas.

"I watched that movie where you played a gay man. You and Cole Hamilton? Man, you guys were hot."

Codi's voice jolted me from my reverie—from my memories of what had come before and what we had to look forward to.

"I think they're going to nominate one or both for an award."

"They've nominated him for a Golden Globe." Pride shone in my voice.

"No shit."

Her voice carried the same note of awe that mine did every time I reflected upon the news. He hadn't wanted to wake up early, but I'd insisted. Good thing I had. The phone had rung non-stop for hours. Cole had my private number and, guessing Peter'd be swamped, had called me. He was genuinely thrilled for Peter, and not the least bit disappointed about not being nominated for their film. That they had nominated him for *Vigilante Justice* eased the sting. Actors playing superheroes in television series rarely received nominations for big awards.

"Yes, shit." I grinned. "And I was damn proud of him."

The cheek I could see reddened. Man, it felt good to tease him. To act like maybe things were normal.

"How long is the trip?"

"On a good day?" She sniffed. "Well, it's about three hundred and fifty kilometers—"

"—two hundred and eighteen miles—" My contribution.

She snickered. "And about four-and-a-half hours. We're behind a plow today and heading against traffic, so that'll all help. But one accident because of some yahoo speeding and crashing, and that'll set us back. Most of the drivers in the Vancouver area have no idea how to drive in snow."

"I thought it was raining."

"Nah, turned to snow a few hours ago. Hell of a mess on the roads, so we're going to take it nice and slow."

"That works." I injected as much assurance as I could. She didn't need to know how stressed we were.

"So what are you all doing in these parts?"

"My family lives in Prince George. We were visiting for Christmas." That felt like a lifetime ago.

"That's sweet. My parents passed years ago and I never married. Being on the road three hundred days a year doesn't lend itself to relationships, you know?"

I did know. When I'd been working on back-to-back projects for the studio, there was little downtime. And since I was in the closet, there were few people I felt safe opening up to. That equaled a lot of lonely nights curled up with a book or a movie and Calvin the orange tabby feline. Oh well, he'd be happy we were home early. Hoped that didn't mess up the pet sitter's schedule. She'd be well-compensated, so that'd help.

"Have you ever considered giving up the open road?"

Codi shot Peter a glance before refocusing her concentration on the road. "Why would I do that? It's all I'm good at."

"Well, there are plenty of jobs in the movie industry. They're always looking for competent drivers. I believe you'd fit that requirement."

I expected an outright rejection, but a heavy silence descended. It lasted so long, I checked my phone again to see if Trinity had texted.

She hadn't.

"You think I could get a job in the movie business?"

"I do." Peter yanked his wallet from his back pocket and rifled through it. He removed a business card. "I'll just put this in your glove box. When you're ready, I can hook you up with a woman named Jo. She runs many of the production vehicles. At the very least I can arrange an introduction."

I didn't miss that he removed every dollar from his wallet and slipped that into the glove box as well. God, I loved him.

My favorite song came on, and I relaxed into my seat. Leslie Odom Junior belted out how he was willing to "Wait for It". Well, I wasn't. Peter and I might have started out as fake boyfriends, but we'd been all-in once we realized this was what we both wanted. Love had come hard, and it'd come fast.

Silence descended in the cab and I stared out the windshield. No snow, but no sun either. We would be in Hope soon enough, and then it was a straight shot to Vancouver. I checked my phone for what felt like the billionth time. Nothing. I considered asking Peter to check his, but that was overkill. If he had a message, he'd see it. Even as I had the thought, he pulled his phone from his pocket and checked it.

Codi pulled into the left lane to pass a slower truck. I wasn't sure about the wisdom of that move given the amount of slush on the road, but this woman knew her stuff and I had to trust in that. I had to put my faith in her.

Peter was putting the phone back in his pocket as it rang. He glanced at Codi. "You mind?"

The music in the cab switched off. "No problem."

Privacy was impossible, but I didn't care. Peter swept and hit the speaker button. "Hey Trinity, we're both here."

"And you're both parents."

The roaring in my ears had me almost missing her next words.

"Baby girl, three pounds, three ounces. Mom and daughter are doing fine. Hailey's asking for you guys."

"Cesarian, right?" Peter's question.

"Yeah. She was conscious through it and they let me stay with her. She was a real trooper. Held it together right until the end then got a little weepy." She paused. "For you guys. She carried on about how awesome it was that the baby was going to have the two best dads ever. I think some of that was the drugs, but most of it was born of love. She loves her baby, but she's good with the plan."

My heart constricted. Just nineteen and facing so many challenges.

Trinity cleared her throat. "You guys know Hailey was hoping to figure out who the father was by looking at the baby."

Which we had all thought unlikely, but she'd held to that belief.

"Anyway, the baby just looks like a baby. She might be Caucasian, or she might be biracial."

"We don't care." Peter's voice was firm. "We never did, and we never will."

"I know. I know." Trinity placated. "It's in Hailey's head that things will be different for her daughter. I can only offer the same assurances you've given over and over."

We didn't care who the father was. Well, if the guy tried to claim his daughter, that was something else. A possibility. One we were prepared to face. But Hailey admitted there had been a few guys. She'd been ashamed, but we hadn't seen it that way. She was a young woman addicted to drugs. She found a way to survive. Her legacy would be this beautiful little girl and, hopefully, sobriety.

"This baby needs a name, you know."

We'd had the discussion several times. But never seriously. We didn't want to presume. We didn't want to jinx it. Turns out we were more superstitious than either had realized.

Peter met my gaze. I nodded.

"Skylar Phoenix Walsh."

My breath caught. The first and middle name we'd figured out, but we'd never discussed the last name. I'd figured we would use Erickson. He was the movie star, of course, and far better-known. I'd accepted that when we'd married. I'd offered to take his name, but he'd declined. It hurt that he hadn't wanted to share his name, but I respected his wishes. Now it all became clear.

"Trinity, did you get that?" My voice trembled.

"I did." There was a murmur in the background. "Hailey says it's the perfect name. She's thrilled."

Which meant the world to me. To us. Hailey would always be a part of our lives, whether she chose an active role or was just a figure in the background. She was the woman who gave us Skylar.

The sign outside indicated we were twenty kilometers outside of Hope.

"We'll be there soon, Trinity."

"We'll be waiting. Travel safe."

The line disconnected.

Codi whistled. "Well, don't that beat all." She punched Peter's shoulder. "You boys are fathers." Her voice turned wistful. "That's, like, a miracle, you know?"

I did. Skylar would face many health challenges ahead, not the least of them being born so tiny. She had us in her corner, though, so I had to believe things would turn out okay. We were already so blessed. I felt greedy asking for one more thing to go our way.

"A miracle." Peter's whisper was reverential. "What...what day is it?"

Our daughter's birthday was my first flippant thought. Then I realized what he was asking. "December 21st."

"The winter solstice." Codi's contribution.

Peter's grin widened. "Our solstice surprise."

"And our solstice blessing." Certainly, we'd never look upon this day the same way again.

Chapter Eight

Peter

We stopped in Chilliwack for a much-needed bathroom break and to regroup, so to speak. After Trinity shared the news, Codi, Thomas, and I settled into a comfortable silence.

Eventually Codi turned the music back on and the tunes had carried us through to the rest stop.

I would've preferred we keep going, but Codi made the call and my bladder was grateful. Now we were out of the higher altitudes, puddles in the pockmarked parking lot surrounded us. Potholes abounded.

"We could hire a taxi from here." I knew we were about an hour and a half out of Vancouver, so well within the range of an adventurous cabbie.

"They'd just have to turn around and come home." Thomas frowned.

"We'd compensate them very well." Money wasn't the issue.

"I..." He kicked a piece of gravel. "I like Codi and she's taken us this far. I mean, I know a taxi would be faster, but I don't want to abandon her, you know?"

I did know. Trust Thomas to put the feelings of others before his own needs. He wasn't wrong.

"Fair enough."

Codi stepped out of the Timmie's with a huge mug of coffee. "Saddle up, boys, we've still got a ways to go."

Before Thomas could say anything, I hauled myself into the backseat. Wasn't as comfortable as the bucket front seat, but it'd do just fine. I didn't want to leave Codi with the impression I thought myself better than my husband.

He glowered but settled into the front seat.

Soon we were pulling out into local traffic first and then back onto the highway. I held my breath as we nearly ran out of shoulder because some yahoo in a sports car wouldn't yield. Christ, were we even going to make it in one piece?

And just as I had that thought, the skies opened up and a downpour hit us. Codi flipped the wipers on and grinned, but her grip on the steering wheel tightened. "I spoke to my dispatcher." She tapped the brakes when a car cut her off, lessening the distance between her and them.

Idiot.

"What did they say?" Thomas's voice was tight.

"I got permission to drive you guys right into Vancouver. It's a straight shot up Broadway, then a left turn and down Oak. You're going to B.C. Women's Hospital, right?"

"We are." The tremor was unmistakable.

"So, it's all set. The client's okay with me being late."

"That's magnanimous of them." I didn't know much about shipping, but I knew on-time delivery was a thing, and there might be penalties. "Is this going to cost you?"

She waved her hand. "Nah. Good reliable drivers are hard to find. This warehouse is fully staffed all the time so if I'm a little late, they won't sweat it. Given how the weather's been, I think they'll just be happy I made it at all."

"What are you carrying? If you don't mind me asking." How had I not thought of this before?

"Toilet paper."

Well, then. I had no idea how to respond to that, and I didn't need to because she flipped the music back on. We were cycling through the musical again, this time landing on George Washington explaining to Alexander Hamilton how "History has its Eyes on You".

I'd been lucky to score tickets to the original production back almost five years ago, and it had blown me away. Taking Thomas with me to the LA production had been the highlight of the trip. He hadn't been enamored of the town. Too glitzy for his tastes. My house had been too big. Everything had been too much. Seeing my life through his eyes made me realize I was okay with giving all that up. Our house in Shaughnessy was perfect.

My phone buzzed with an incoming text. Yanking it from my pocket, I swiped, and my breath whooshed out.

Our little girl.

The knitted cap on her head was tiny and pink. She was swaddled in a pink blanket with her eyes closed. So small. So precious.

Choking back threatening tears, I passed the phone to Thomas.

His gasp was audible. He met my gaze and his eyes shimmered. "She's perfect."

"She is."

"That a picture of your daughter?" Codi's question pulled us from the moment of shared intimacy.

"Yeah."

"Well, the first light we stop at, you'll have to show me. If you don't mind."

Mind? I owed this woman everything. "Happy to share."

"That's great." Her grin, what I could see of it, anyway, was unrepentant. "I got five nieces, two nephews, and a great-niece." She titled her chin. "I love all the kids. I especially love being able to give them back at the end of the day."

A sentiment I used to echo. I'd never had a yearning for a child on my own until I met Thomas. Suddenly having a family had meant everything. And it hadn't mattered how we were going to do it—we were going to become parents. We were going to share our good fortune. And our love. Always our love.

****

There was no exit for Broadway. Just a shot off the Grandview Highway, a dip down Boundary road, a left on Broadway, and we were heading into the city. We hit a red light at the intersection and Codi took a long look at the photo. She cooed.

Much the same as I had.

Traffic was heavy, given it was the tail end of rush hour on a dark-and-rainy Friday night. For many people, this was the official beginning of the holiday season and apparently everyone was on the road.

When *Hamilton* ended, Codi had selected, of all things, *Oklahoma*. I did my companions a favor by not singing along, but Thomas shot me a glance, assuring me he hadn't forgotten. On our first date, I'd told him about how being the lead in Oklahoma had changed the trajectory of my life. From small-town Texas to the big bright lights of LA, and now to Vancouver, Canada. My life had taken me through many places and introduced me to many people, but Thomas would always be the most important.

"We're coming up to West 29th."

Codi's words brought me out of my reverie.

"It's just past six, so I can legally park on the street. I'll pull over, and you guys hop out."

"I don't know how to thank you." And I didn't. The paltry few hundred in the glove box didn't feel like nearly enough.

"You boys be good fathers to that little girl, and that's all the thanks I'll ever need."

A thought occurred. "You have my card. Text me and I'll send you a baby picture. If you'd like." I shouldn't be presumptuous. Not everyone wanted pics of someone else's kid.

"I'd love it. And I promise I won't leak it."

That thought had never occurred to me. I often had to make snap judgements about people, and even back in Cache Creek, I'd known Codi was good people. I spotted the sign for the cross-street as the truck glided to a stop. Thomas hopped out and I handed him our suitcases. On impulse I gave Codi a peck to the cheek before exiting the cab. The light turned green, and we sprinted across, waving to Codi with one hand while carrying our suitcases in the other.

Belatedly I realized we'd left the thermal container and the mugs. Oh well, nothing to be done about it now. The light changed again, and we crossed as Codi pulled out into traffic. My breath caught for a moment. I owed her everything.

"You okay?" Thomas' brow was furrowed in concern.

"Yeah...just hoping she'll call, you know? I would love her to be in our lives somehow."

"So we give Jo the heads-up and hopefully something will work out. Even if it doesn't, I suspect you're going to get a text asking for baby pictures."

He was all smiles.

Right.

I nodded and he gestured for us cross the parking lot. A couple dozen steps weren't enough time to get nervous, and soon we entered the hospital. After using the hand sanitizer, we followed Trinity's directions to the maternity ward.

"This is surreal."

Thomas' words echoed my thoughts as we rode the elevator up. Surreal indeed.

When we exited the elevator, I glanced over, and there sat Trinity. She was engrossed in her phone and didn't notice us. I approached cautiously, careful to make plenty of noise to alert her of our presence. Thomas' boot squeaked, and she looked up. Her expression morphed from curiosity to happiness in a microsecond.

"You two are a sight for sore eyes."

A little clichéd, but we had been on the road for almost twenty hours with almost no sleep. I was grateful we were still upright.

"How are they?" I glanced at Thomas whose face wore every line of worry he'd endured.

"Resting comfortably." Trinity tucked her cell phone in the back pocket of her jeans. "Why don't we sit?"

I didn't want to sit. I'd been sitting for the better part of a day and I wanted action. I wanted to be doing something. Of course, this wasn't my show. I wasn't in charge, as much as I wanted to be. I took Thomas' hand and we sat on the padded bench while Trinity took the seat across from us.

"Start with Hailey." Thomas' words were gentle. "Is she okay?"

Trinity tilted her head in contemplation. "I used the word trooper, right? And that fits. She's been through a lot in the past twenty-four hours, and the emotions have, at times, overtaken her. I think she feels guilty about having left the apartment, although that might have turned out to be a good thing because she was with people when she nearly passed out. I've assured her she's done a great job, and no one faults her."

"Of course not." I whispered the words.

"But she also knew how important carrying the baby to term was and being early has distressed her." Trinity rubbed at an invisible crease in her jeans. "She also knows her addiction will have ramifications for Skylar, and that's more guilt."

"Is there anything we can do?" Thomas squeezed my hand.

"Reassure her. Be supportive. She seems genuine in her desire to turn her life around and you paying for her to go to a special rehab center is going to help."

I nodded. Eternal Springs was up near Hope and had a great reputation with a low relapse rate. Hailey would stay as long as she needed. At least here my money came in handy.

"How will she cope?" Thomas scratched his head.

"They're going to keep her on methadone for now, but she'll head to detox when she's ready. I won't lie, it won't be an easy road. She's in for a lifetime battle with addiction." Trinity's dark eyes were somber. "She gets it. Maybe better than others I've seen. At least I hope she does. Relapse might cost her more than just any progress she's made."

Death. Addicts died. Some didn't, but many did. A future too painful to contemplate.

Trinity tucked a lock of her black hair behind her ear. "So, on to Skylar." A small smile appeared. "She's a good weight for being early.

Her lungs aren't fully developed, so she's going to stay in the neonatal intensive care unit for a few days at least."

"And the drugs?"

Tension radiated off my husband. I tightened my grip on his hand.

"From Hailey's drug use, they've diagnosed Neonatal Abstinence Syndrome. But we expected that." She rushed the words. "And they have a good account of the drugs Hailey's taken, so that's all good. Skylar will receive ever-decreasing doses of the methadone and eventually they should be able to wean her off completely." She met my gaze and then focused on Thomas. "This was all expected. She's jaundiced, and that's being treated. She has had no seizures, and they settled her, so that's all good. But you know this is early days."

"And she'll cry more. Have trouble sleeping. Throw up or have diarrhea. Runny nose and fever and problems feeding..." He listed off the symptoms. "I get all of that. And part of me is glad I've never raised kids before so I won't know what normal looks like. She'll just be..." He scrubbed his face with his hand. "I'm terrified, Trinity, but I know we can do this. I mean we have to, right? And we'll have the nurse and plenty of check-ups so..." Pain etched his face.

"They'll make sure she isn't suffering." Trinity's words were soft. "But yes, she's going to be a challenging baby. You have the patience and love to withstand any trials." She met his gaze but shot a glance over to me as well. "They'll monitor her closely. And she might turn out to be a healthy little girl."

"Or she might have health issues. But we'll deal." I could stand by those words with conviction. The professionals had informed us of all of this. We'd talked it out. And I also knew nothing could prepare us for the reality, but we were in this together.

When Trinity rose, we followed. She took us over to the nurses' station and registration desk where they explained protocols to us and then gave us parent bracelets. Yeah, this shit was getting real.

Trinity stood at the door and waited for both of us to nod.

We followed her down a long corridor and eventually to a room.

The door was half-ajar, and the room was dark.

She knocked.

"Come in."

The voice was groggy, but I'd know Hailey anywhere. She often reverted to what the psychologist termed little-girl mode. Her voice would go high, and she'd twist her hands and not make eye contact. Other times she was mature beyond her years, making demands, issuing commands, and making her needs and wants known. I preferred those times because that young woman knew what she wanted and that included us parenting her child.

Trinity entered first and Thomas followed, then I brought up the rear.

Hailey was tiny in the enormous bed. She was a petite woman to begin with—barely five feet tall—but this bed diminished her further. Made her appear fragile.

"How are you feeling?" Trinity's words were quiet as she approached the bed.

Hailey pressed a hand to her still-distended belly. "It hurts."

"Do you need more meds?" A dangerous question to ask an addict, but none of us wanted her suffering.

She shook her head. "They're going to give me something to help me sleep, and then tomorrow they're going to get me up and moving." She stuck her lower lip out. "I don't want to move. I just want to stay curled up."

Trinity now stepped close to the bedside. "I'm sure you do, but you agreed the doctors know best."

Hailey didn't appear pleased, but she strained to look around Trinity, seemingly pleased when she spotted Thomas and myself. "Have you seen her yet?"

When Thomas didn't answer, I pulled his hand into mine and said, "Not yet. We wanted to make sure you were okay first." We owed her that much.

"I'm fine." More pouting. "I want you to go take care of Skylar. Pretty name."

"Pretty name for a pretty baby." Trinity shifted. "You get some rest, okay?"

"So I'll be nice and rested for rehab."

Ah, there was the Hailey I knew.

Steely determination crossed her expression. "I'm going to be the best patient they've ever had."

"I'm sure you will." Thomas scratched his head. "Whatever you need...you let us know, okay?"

Hailey gestured to the flowers and a teddy bear on the bedside table. "You guys take good care of me."

Trinity shot me a glance that warned me to hold my tongue. I hadn't sent flowers, and I was pretty sure Thomas hadn't had time either. Well, if the social worker had thought it appropriate, I was appreciative.

"We'll let you get some sleep." Thomas squeezed my hand. "And we'll go and see the baby." The hitch in his voice was unmistakable, and it matched the stutter in my heart.

Hailey's eyes drooped, but she still reached out her hands.

On instinct, Thomas and I moved forward, each taking one.

She squeezed. "I love the name you picked for her. And I know you'll love her and protect her, and that's all I can really ask for." Her eyes shimmered. "Thank you."

"No, thank you." Thomas placed his other hand over hers, encasing it. "We'll love her, but she'll always know about you. We won't forget you."

I wasn't sure those were the right words, but something seemed to settle in Hailey and when she pulled her hands back, we let them go. I took Thomas' hand in mine and we waved then slowly backed out of the room.

Hailey's eyes were already closed.

Chapter Nine

Thomas

It took entirely too much time before we were able to get to Skylar. We had to register and wait for photos to be taken. We had to sign releases. Then we moved to the handwashing station. We'd ditched our coats and sweaters. We rolled up our sleeves past the elbow, removed our wedding rings, then scrubbed our hands, especially under the fingernails, and arms as if our lives depended on it. Well, our daughter's life did depend on it, so we did it without complaint.

Finally, they led us into a large room and over to a crib in a dark corner of the room. She was so tiny. Breathtakingly and heart-stoppingly so.

The nurse, Bryan, encouraged us to touch her.

I stroked her soft cheek and couldn't stop the tears.

Peter took her tiny hand in his, gently touching each finger in reverence. Tears brimmed in his eyes but didn't fall.

We hadn't planned on Skylar, but she was the best thing in our lives.

"Tomorrow, we'll be able to have you hold her skin-to-skin. That contact is so healing for the little ones." Bryan gave us encouragement, then stepped away to give us a little privacy.

The thought of holding someone so tiny terrified me. I had so little experience with babies, and Peter had confided he had little either. Well, we'd learn. I'd read about the skin-to-skin thing and would gladly do it. Bonding. A chance to interact and bond with our daughter.

Peter yawned into his sleeve.

In sympathy, a wave of exhaustion rolled over me. It was going on eight at night, and it felt like it'd been days since we'd been asleep. Heck, only twenty-four hours ago I'd been recovering from telling my family the truth. That was a distant memory.

I pulled out my phone and snapped several photos.

Peter leaned over to press a kiss to Skylar's forehead.

I did the same.

Bryan was there within moments. "She's in excellent hands, and I have your contact information. I'll call if anything happens."

If she took a turn. If something bad happened. I didn't want to think about it but that was the reality we faced. Someone so fragile. My heart.

My daughter. Our daughter.

With reluctance, we headed out.

Trinity was there beyond the doors, watching over our clothes and suitcases. She hovered as we put our coats on. "I'll give you a lift."

Peter's refusal was automatic. "We can take a cab."

"I know you can, but you're going to accept a ride from me, and we'll talk."

More talking? Well, if this was what Trinity wanted, we wouldn't argue.

I secured my cap, but Peter stuffed his tuque in his suitcase. I grinned. Vain to the end. We escaped into the winter's night only to be assaulted by the rain coming down heavy and cold.

None of us had umbrellas, so it was a sprint to Trinity's car. We secured our suitcases in the trunk and I dove for the backseat before Peter could argue. I might've been taller, but I was also younger. Easier for me to contort myself. In the end I didn't need to. Trinity's Mazda was quite roomy.

She hit the defrost and cleared the condensation from the window before heading out to Oak Street. Having been to our house several times over the past few months, she knew the way.

In the end, there were no discussions. No words were spoken.

Ha, clever woman. The promise of ponderings never emerged. She'd effectively manipulated us into hitching a ride with her. One we never would have agreed to otherwise. Although not far out of her way, Shaughnessy was in the opposite direction from Mission City.

When she pulled into our driveway, she cut the engine. "You guys are incredibly brave to take this on, but I have no doubt Hailey made the right decision when she chose you."

"And Eternal Springs is ready for her, right?"

Peter's question mirrored my own thoughts. They would care for Hailey. We'd see to it.

Trinity nodded. "They're keeping her in hospital longer than they normally would for a woman having a C-section, but when she's stable, she'll head up to Hope. I'm driving her myself. She wanted it that way."

And I had little doubt Trinity was happier with that decision. She was fiercely protective of her charge.

"You guys need to get some rest. You're in for plenty of stress for the next few weeks."

"Until she's eighteen I think," I said, weariness in my voice.

Trinity snickered. "Yeah, that's about right. Lots of sleepless nights between now and then."

"Worth every moment." Peter yawned again.

Patting his knee, Trinity met my gaze in the rearview mirror. "You'll do good."

Assurance I hadn't realized I needed. "Thank you."

She popped the trunk. "My pleasure. I wish all my clients had a happy ending."

But this wasn't the end. Not for Skylar and definitely not for Hailey.

We got out of Trinity's car, grabbed our suitcases from the trunk, and headed up to the front porch. The rain was still coming down in torrents and we shook ourselves off as Trinity backed out of the driveway. I waved as she drove away.

Before either or us could retrieve our keys, the front door opened.

Janee stood there, Calvin cuddled in her arms. He glanced at me, eyed Peter, then snuggled back into Janee's embrace.

Peter choked on a laugh. He scratched behind Calvin's ear before Janee stepped aside and we entered the front foyer. In mere moments we'd shed our coats and had them hanging on the hooks. I hung up the cap and we both sat on the bench to unlace our boots.

"Not that I'm not happy to see you two, but care to explain?"

I'd known Janee for years through the movie business, and her love of animals had always been clear.

But her condo didn't allow pets. Not even goldfish. In the past, Janee let everyone know she was available to pet sit anytime. She'd watch kids, but pets were her jam. She was also saving money to buy a condo that allowed pets, so this cat-sitting opportunity had come at the perfect time.

Peter refused to tell me how much he was paying, but I suspected there would be a hefty tip involved.

"We had to come home." Peter glanced at me, raising his eyebrows.

I tucked my boots under the bench and made my way over to my recalcitrant cat. A few scritches behind the ear and he purred. When I held open my arms, he deigned to climb into them. "It's still a secret, but we're adopting a baby, and she was born earlier today. Early." I stuck my nose in Calvin's fur, seeking solace. "We raced down here so we could see the baby and her mother."

Janee's green eyes shone. "Adopting a baby? Oh, that is just like the two of you. Pleasantly domesticated."

I wasn't sure how to respond to that so I opted not to.

"I'm going to run and pack my bag so I can get out of your hair."

"You're welcome to stay..." Peter's words were said to Janee's back as she was already running up the stairs. He turned to me.

I shrugged. "There might be a guy, and I told her she could have him visit, but she'd never do that."

"No, she wouldn't."

Calvin swatted at my face and I let him down. He twined himself between Peter's legs then headed off toward the kitchen.

Peter arched an eyebrow. "Is that a hint?"

I laughed. "He's not known for his subtlety."

Before I could follow my formerly feral cat, Peter yanked me in for a hard kiss. "I'll call Janee a taxi. How about you warm up a shower for us?"

With the size of our hot water tank, it'd take about five seconds for the hot water to hit, but I understood his meaning. "Calvin's stomach, then shower."

He winked.

I made my way to the spotless kitchen where Calvin sat. On the counter. I glared and he indolently licked a paw. Yeah, I knew who really ran this house. Pulling out a couple of treats, I put them in his empty food bowl. The one on the floor.

He glared, his eyes slowly blinking.

I shrugged.

Finally he tipped his chin but leapt down to the floor. Within moments the treats were consumed.

"And don't come into the bedroom. I have...plans."

As if he understood me, he headed to his very expensive cat bed in the family room which he would ignore in favor of the very expensive leather couch. He hadn't clawed it, so for that I was grateful.

I could hear Peter and Janee on the front porch, so I made a beeline for the stairs and took them two at a time up to the upper landing. Within moments, I was in our bedroom and stripping. Rumpled sweater and the stinky shirt hit the floor, soon followed by my socks, jeans, and underwear. I could clean tomorrow.

I stopped only for a piss before hitting the shower. As soon as the temperature was hot, I stepped under the spray.

Bliss.

Over the noise of the water I heard the bathroom door close and within moments the toilet flushed and the water stuttered. Ah, great minds.

Peter opened the shower door and let himself in. Steam rose and he stepped under the head across from where I was.

I poured body wash on my hand and lathered it up, approaching him slowly. His grin was all the permission I needed. I leisurely explored his body from his chest to his underarms, down his sides, across his belly, and lower still.

He stilled my hand, then reached for the bottle. "My turn."

No lasciviousness tainted his voice. Our eyes met as he placed his hand on my chest.

Heat suffused me, hotter even than the water. As he washed me with his right hand, he placed his left behind my head and tugged me down for a kiss. The meeting of our mouths was as unhurried as his movements. Slow. Gentle.

I groaned. "I want you to make love to me but I'm so tired."

He nuzzled my neck. "I'm feeling the same way." He poured a bit of body wash in his hand and grasped our cocks. "Hold on."

Deciding to take him literally, I placed my hands on the cold, tiled wall. I had been semi-erect when we started, but him grasping me with such strength kicked my libido into high gear. As he slid his fist up and down our cocks, I thought of the first time we'd showered together. My first time with a man. My first time with anyone.

"I'm close." I pushed the words out between gritted teeth. I arched into his touch and gave myself up to the sensation. Nothing existed except him and me. Right here. Right now.

Despite being close, the actual orgasm snuck up on me, but then hit me hard. I gasped.

Peter said, "Oh, thank fuck." Soon he was spurting.

Our semen mixed, carried away by the hot water.

I wanted nothing more than to fall into a heap on the floor, but bed was a siren's call I couldn't ignore. While he caught his breath, I grabbed the shampoo. I turned his pliant body, making it easier to lather his hair. I dug my fingers into his scalp as he sighed. This was one of the most intimate things we did for each other, and when the shampoo was rinsed out, I pinched his gorgeous ass. "You go get into bed. I'll join you."

He glanced over his shoulder and whatever he saw in my expression, he read it correctly and nodded as he exited the shower.

I needed a moment. He accepted that with grace, and that warmed me even more. Our intimacy never ceased to surprise me. To please me. To evoke gratitude within me. As I washed my hair, the events of the past twenty-four hours cascaded down around me. This was my life.

Peter. My parents. Sarah. Skylar. And Hailey, to a degree. Six months ago, I'd felt completely alone. Then I'd met a beautiful man and my entire life changed. It wasn't the external beauty that'd drawn me. It'd been his loneliness. Amazingly, two souls in desperate need of connection found each other in the maelstrom of the movie business.

I shut off the water and stepped onto the heated tiles. This house might appear average on the outside, but they'd kitted it out with every possible amenity. And often I felt guilty, but tonight I had only gratitude. I toweled myself dry and padded into our bedroom.

Peter had plugged in our phones by our respective bedsides and he lay in the middle of the bed, holding up the blanket.

I eased myself in and let him pull me into his arms.

"I sent texts to your parents and Sarah. I promised we would call in the morning."

"I should do that now—"

He tightened his grip. "Your mother texted back right away and said tomorrow was fine. She said to tell you not to fret. That was her word—fret. Because she knows you. We need to let go tonight because tomorrow is the beginning of the rest of our lives and it'll be here soon enough."

His understanding of me never ceased to amaze.

He pressed a kiss to the back of my neck.

"I'm tired but I'm also wired, you know?"

"I do." A chuckle rumbled in his chest. "And part of me wants to get up and shop because we don't have any baby things."

Oh my god. "You just had to bring that up." We both claimed to be rational men, but we were also both highly superstitious. We hadn't wanted to bring any baby items into the house and jinx us. Now we faced an infant coming home in a few weeks but we had nothing prepared. Of course, with Peter's money, we could easily have the entire room furnished by the end of tomorrow. Huh. Something to consider.

"At least the room is painted." The previous owner had painted the nursery a bright yellow with animals on two walls. Funny, we never considered redecorating. We faithfully believed this day would come.

"Is this real?" The tremor carried through my words.

"I have photos on my camera to prove they're real. Oh, I hope you don't mind, but I sent one to your mom."

"Mind? You realize what you've started?"

His hand on my chest tightened. "What?"

"My mom is becoming a grandmother."

"True..." The hesitancy in his voice rang clear.

"I just..." What was I trying to say? "I never thought I'd be the one to give that to her, you know?"

"Because you were in the closet." He flexed his fingers. "Well, I never planned to have kids, so this is a shock for me too." Before I could say anything, he continued, "and just because I hadn't planned on it, doesn't mean I don't want it. You didn't have to twist my arm, Thomas. I'm just as excited as you are."

How had he known? "More like nervous, terrified, and panicked."

"I know how to relieve some of that stress..."

"Uh, maybe not while I'm thinking about Skylar."

He barked out a laugh. "Thomas, if we don't have sex because of our daughter, it's going to be a very long dry spell."

"Well, when you put it like that." I brought his hand up to my mouth and grazed a kiss to his knuckles. "Just maybe when both the body and mind are willing."

"I can wait." He settled the duvet and the darkness engulfed us.

This was our new life. Pretty fricking amazing. And he was right—we could handle this. As long as we were together, we could take on the world. This was what love gave. The power to believe in the impossible and to make it come true.

His breathing evened out, and eventually mine did as well.

Epilogue

Peter

"Just one more step, sweetheart. You can do it. Come to Grandpa."

I watched my daughter take tentative steps toward my father-in-law and cherished the sight. A year. She'd been born a year ago today. If she managed the few steps on her own, this would be a new milestone. She'd hit plenty of them—some on time, some a little behind, and one or two earlier than expected. Every day brought something new and wondrous.

"How's Hailey doing?" Norma's soft words were for me alone.

"She's good. We couldn't get her to come today. She's good with randomly dropping by now and then, but can't handle the specific dates, you know?" The young woman was studying at the University of British Columbia after earning her high school diploma in the spring. She lived on campus and had chosen to stay there over Christmas as she didn't have anywhere else to go. As usual, she declined our invitation to stay with us. I hoped she might appear at some point over the holidays.

"I'd like to meet her."

That was probably one of the reasons the young woman was staying away. When she knew it was just Thomas and me, she was okay. The thought of running into anyone else made her uncomfortable. I didn't blame her.

"Mom, I think the roast is done."

Thomas speak for 'help me'. He'd been intransigent about cooking tonight. Norma offered, of course, but Thomas wanted to show off his culinary skills. His mother was subtly checking his efforts at every turn, so we weren't likely to get food poisoning. My husband's efforts in the kitchen were laudable, but the results were occasionally questionable.

"That's my good girl." Bart pulled Skylar into his arms and swept her high, eliciting delighted giggles.

Sarah clapped.

Thomas stepped from the kitchen, looking distressed. "What did I miss?"

"Your daughter's first unassisted steps."

His face fell at my words. Before I could point out there would be plenty more times, Sarah had her camera in her brother's face.

"Don't worry, I recorded it."

He watched the screen with rapt attention, his grin widening. As the video ended, he looked up and met my gaze.

I mouthed *I love you* to him.

He blushed.

"Dada."

My cue. I held open my arms and Bart placed Skylar in them. She reached for my beard and tugged. If I hadn't been on a short hiatus, I'd have considered shaving it off. Our daughter had grabby hands.

She glanced around and spotted Thomas. "Papa."

He held up the oven mitts as a shield.

If he took her in his arms, we'd never get fed. "I'll put her in her high chair."

"And I'll cut up some avocados," Sarah offered.

Nothing Skylar loved more than that particular item. She'd adore her Aunt Sarah for giving it to her. Our daughter was nothing if not gracious. Especially when she had mushed avocado in her hair.

"I should set the table." Bart glanced at the elegant, expensive, and empty dining room table.

"We're eating in the kitchen." Norma threaded her arm through his and tugged him toward the kitchen.

Thomas and I'd discussed using the dining room. We would for Christmas dinner, but tonight was family, and family sat at the kitchen table.

Sarah held her arms wide and Skylar pushed away from me and toward her waiting aunt. Her black hair ruffled a bit before Sarah smoothed it down. "Avocados?"

Our daughter nodded enthusiastically, her blue eyes alight. So easily bribed.

Alone for a moment, I inhaled deeply. Pine from the Christmas tree, spices from the roast, and something less tangible. Something ethereal. This was to be our daughter's second Christmas and just remembering she'd spent her first one in the hospital was enough to constrict my lungs. Every day was a gift. Every day a reminder what a lucky bastard I really was.

****

Thomas

Some nights Skylar would lie in her crib and talk to herself. The girl never stopped, and she'd go on and on until she suddenly dropped into sleep. Other nights she was asleep by the time her head hit the pillow. Fortunately, tonight was one of those nights.

My parents were settled in the guest room at the other end of the hall, and Sarah was ensconced in the in-law suite over the garage, claiming she wanted privacy. I had a sneaking suspicion my sister had a boyfriend who was down in Vancouver for Christmas. And as much as I didn't want to think about her having sex, at least I knew where she was. She had a good head on her shoulders. Maybe one day she'd introduce us to the young man.

I came out of the bathroom into the bedroom to find Peter scrolling on his phone. Wearing his reading glasses. He caught sight of me, whipped them off, and dropped them into the open drawer of his bedside table. I sauntered over to his side of the bed and snagged them, holding them up to the light. "You know, I never thought glasses were sexy, but I want to fuck you every time I see you in them."

He scoffed and reached for them.

I held them just out of reach for another moment before handing them back.

He snagged a cloth and cleaned them, muttering something about fingerprints.

Truth was, he didn't like to be reminded that he was getting older. His latest job was a recurring role in a television series. As the mentor. He loved the part, but truly disliked the fact his wrinkles and lines were emphasized rather than minimized. That and they made him grow—and keep—the beard. He still had plenty of leading roles to take on, but for now the role of wise older man suited him. And with such a small part, he was home most of the time, which was good, because I was shooting the third season of *Vigilante Justice*. That kept me pretty busy.

Rounding the bed, I plugged in my phone. "Did Sarah send you the video?"

"She did." Peter chuckled. "And I've forwarded it to Codi. She sent back a flurry of emojis." The honorary grandmother worked on the set of *VJ* with me. She had no regrets about giving up her big rig and settling into the role of driver on a movie set.

I slid into bed next to him and curled against his side. "I'm exhausted."

"Cooking will do that."

I pinched his side and he snickered. "I worked hard on that meal."

"And the roast was definitely well-cooked."

"You mean shoe-leather tough." I winced mentally.

"Except the parts that dripped in blood. Quite remarkable how you managed to cook it so...unevenly."

I wanted to poke him in the ribs again, but his teasing lightened my heart. Everyone had graciously eaten the roast, ever so grateful my mom had made apple pie for dessert. We had it with ice cream, of course. No Tiger tail to be seen. I wasn't sharing my stash with anyone who didn't appreciate the flavor as much as I did.

"I should probably warn you."

Peter's tone was light but his words tightened my gut.

"Sarah is making noises about being a surrogate for us when she's finished with her doctorate. Something about Skylar needing a sibling."

"Oh my god." My sister was nothing if not relentless. Yet I paused. "You realize that means you'll be the sperm donor." Well, maybe that wouldn't be so bad. A son or daughter running around with sea-green eyes.

"Or we can adopt another child in need."

"Or both."

"Oh my god." Horror filled his voice, but so did awe.

A part-time nanny helped us out. I could cut back on my work to spend more time at home. I worked because I wanted to be viewed as an equal partner. The past year had proved I didn't need to stress so much. Peter had never once treated me as less than. Seeing our daughter more held great appeal. "We have time to decide. Sarah's got three years left in her program."

My husband let out a sign of relief. "Fair enough."

A moment of stillness crept over the room.

"Today ranks up there with one of the best days ever."

"True." I measured my words carefully. "But then so does every day since I met you. I..." I swallowed. "I didn't know life could be so amazing."

"It could be even more amazing."

He was serious? Because I couldn't think of a single thing missing in our lives.

"How so?"

He rolled on top of me, pinning me to the mattress. "We could make love."

Fatigue fled. "I like the sound of that."

And he proceeded to cherish me, taking me to the heights of pleasure and ensuring we had a very wonderful winter solstice.

Want to know what happens next? Peter and Thomas are back to support their friend, Val Langford, as he struggles to put his life back together after a catastrophe in his professional life. Check out *Valentino in Vancouver.*

Here's a sneak peek:

I was having a spectacularly bad day when I turned up at my buddy's house in Vancouver, Canada, cap in hand.

Oh, who was I kidding? Bad day, bad week, bad month...it all blended together at this point. Had it only been three weeks since my world came crashing down around me? I didn't need to check my phone to know the date. Three weeks on the nose. And I'd run. All the way from Los Angeles to Canada. Didn't feel far enough away, this still being the Pacific Coast. I should've gone to London or Johannesburg or, best of all, Siberia. No internet and cell phones on the tundra.

Right?

Hoping my disheveled appearance wouldn't get me turfed back to the street, I rang the bell. I'd optimistically sent away the taxi driver.

But I had pocketed a card from the company, so summoning one back shouldn't be too tough. Where I'd go, though, I had no idea. Some hotels took cash. And looked the other way.

Or maybe my downfall hadn't been covered in the media up here. Maybe I was making myself out to be more important than I actually was.

Delusional.

No, chances were Vancouver had seen some of the coverage. I'd been responsible for sending many television and movie productions up this way. At least the industry rags would've mentioned me. Now I had a Canadian stamp in my treasured passport and desperation in my heart.

I rang the bell again.

God, what if he wasn't home? What if he was off shooting somewhere? He'd done a film in the Yukon last year, although he'd mostly stuck close to Vancouver since then. But what was to say he hadn't flown the coop?

The door opened, and my heart sank.

Instead of my buddy Peter, I was facing his husband, Thomas. Thomas, who'd never quite warmed to me. Thomas, who kept a protective stance around Peter. Thomas, whose leg currently barred my entry.

"What do you want, Val?"

"Papa?" A little voice came from behind him, and a little head emerged from between his legs, poking her head out.

Her? Yes, right, Peter and Thomas had a daughter. Almost two years old, if my memory was correct.

She pointed to me. "Stranger."

Thomas ruffled her hair, then pulled her into his arms. "Yes, Skylar, stranger." He kissed her cherubic cheek. "He has about ten seconds to tell me why he's here before I close the door in his face."

His tone was singsongy and sweet. I caught the underlying bite.

Valentino In Vancouver

Hiding out may be the hottest thing he's ever done.

Val

When I need to get away from the heat in Los Angeles, I head to a friend's house in Vancouver, Canada. I just need to hide out. Oh, and that cute redhead? A mighty fine way to pass the time. Will this fling become something more by the time things cool down?

Seamus

When I'm invited to my boss's house for a party, I'm thrilled. And nervous. Then I meet a guy who helps me relax. Even when I find out who he is, I keep coming back for more. Only it turns out I might be way over my head. Can I get out before I fall for him?

Buy it here!

And want to discover the story of how Peter and Thomas from *Solstice Surprise* met? Check out *Catch a Tiger by the Tail*.

Catch a Tiger by the Tail

Thomas Walsh knows the number one rule in the film industry. Don't get involved with the talent. But resisting the urge to take the big screen to the bedroom can be hell when the lead actor on the set looks good enough to eat...one slow lick at a time.

Peter Erickson's latest role as a gay man hits a little too close to home. He's still in the closet and secretly grieving the death of his lover. Then an enchanting production assistant catches his eye, and he's surprised by the instant attraction that stirs more than his wounded soul.

When the two men are caught on camera in a very intimate pose, both Thomas and Peter are afraid they've caught a tiger by the tail.

Catch a Tiger by the Tail
Available from all retailers.

Want another Christmas story? With a grumpy ginger lumberjack Scrooge and a sunny pediatric nurse? Check out *Ginger Snapping All the Way*.

Maddox

I'm not a fan of Christmas. I'm happy to stay up in my mountain cabin and let the silly season pass me by. But when a friend asks for a favor, I can't say no. Now I'm stuck in my cabin during a snowstorm, trapped with the most beautiful man I've ever met—who can't wait to get away. He just might break my heart when he goes.

Ravi

I'm racing to get home for the birth of my goddaughter when mechanical troubles force my plane's emergency landing. There are no beds at the inn due to a horrendous storm, but a friend says she knows a guy who won't mind putting me up until the bad weather passes. Now I'm trapped with that man, and I must decide if I stay, hiding from the rest of the world, or go and face my past to earn a shot at my happily ever after.

This is a 72k word, hurt/comfort, lumberjack/nurse, grumpy/sunshine, forced proximity MM romance novel with a moderate amount of angst.

Buy it here!

Also available:
Ginger Snapping All the Way (Love in Mission City Book 1)
Stanley's Christmas Redemption (Love in Mission City Book 2)
Sleigh Bells and Second Chances (Love in Mission City Book 3)
Love in Mission City: The Boyfriends Duet

Love in Mission City: The Shorts
Page Against the Machine
The Lightkeeper's Love Affair
Ace's Place
Marcus's Cadence
Not in it for the Money
The Beauty of the Beast
Axe to Grind
Grindstone's Edge
Hugh (Single Dads of Gaynor Beach)
Anthony (Single Dads of Gaynor Beach)
Xavier (Single Dads of Gaynor Beach)
Love Furever (Friends of Gaynor Beach Animal Rescue)
Husky Love (Friends of Gaynor Beach Animal Rescue)
My Past, Your Future
If Only for Today
Catch a Tiger by the Tail
You See Me
Sun, Surf, and Surprises
Love Without Reservations
An Uncommon Gentleman
Caressa's Homecoming (Bound by Love Book 1)
Cole's Reckoning (Bound by Love Book 2)

Audiobooks
Ginger Snapping All the Way
Stanley's Christmas Redemption
Love in Mission City: The Shorts

Page Against the Machine
The Lightkeeper's Love Affair
Ace's Place
Marcus's Cadence
Not in it for the Money
My Past, Your Future
If Only for Today
Catch a Tiger by the Tail
Solstice Surprise
An Uncommon Gentleman

Want a free short story? The story is set in Gaynor Beach, California where there are plenty of single dads and puppy rescues! You can sign up for my newsletter so you can keep up with all the great stuff I'm doing as well as pictures of my own pooches, Ally and Finnegan.

Hemingway's Happy Day
https://dl.bookfunnel.com/dehfylgwsy

Interested in knowing more about Gabbi?

Sign up for her newsletter
Follow her on Bookbub
Follow her on Instagram

USA Today Bestselling author Gabbi Grey lives in beautiful British Columbia where her fur baby chin-poo keeps her safe from the nasty neighborhood squirrels. Working for the government by day, she spends her early mornings writing contemporary, gay, sweet, and dark erotic BDSM romances. While she firmly believes in happy endings, she also believes in making her characters suffer before finding their true love. She also writes m/f romances as Gabbi Black and Gabbi Powell.